Maisey Yates is a *New York Times* bestselling author of over seventy-five romance novels. She has a coffee habit she has no interest in kicking, and a slight Pinterest addiction. She lives with her husband and children in the Pacific Northwest. When Maisey isn't writing she can be found singing in the grocery store, shopping for shoes online and probably not doing dishes. Check out her website: maiseyyates.com.

CROWNING HIS CONVENIENT PRINCESS

MAISEY YATES

MILLS & BOON

First Published in Great Britain 2019
by Mills & Boon, an imprint of HarperCollins*Publishers*
1 London Bridge Street, London, SE1 9GF

© 2019 Maisey Yates

ISBN: 978-0-263-08667-6

MIX
Paper from
responsible sources
FSC˚ C007454

This book is produced from independently certified FSC™ paper
to ensure responsible forest management.
For more information visit www.harpercollins.co.uk/green.

Printed and bound in Great Britain

For Mr. H, my 4th and 5th Grade teacher. I remember you teaching us about pseudonyms, and you said if we didn't use one you might be able to find us and read our books someday if we ever became authors. Unless we wrote romance, which you didn't read. Now you're mentioned in a romance—bet you didn't see that coming.

CHAPTER ONE

LATIKA BAKSHMI TOOK a deep breath before steeling herself to open the door. She knew exactly what she would find behind it.

Or rather, *who*.

Prince Gunnar von Bjornland, her boss's brother, dissolute rake, and general disgrace to his country. A man she despised with every fiber of her being. And, a man who was her current project.

Queen Astrid, who was not just her boss, but also her friend and confidant, had asked her to take on the task of reforming Gunnar, and she was going to do it.

In a minute.

"Stop lurking outside my door."

She jolted. "How did you know I was outside the door?"

The door swung open, revealing a man who was more Viking God than mere mortal. His blond hair was pushed back from his face, a slightly darker beard covering his jaw. His light blue eyes were the color of ice, but somehow contained heat nonetheless.

And his *body*.

It was an assault to all her good sense and she hated and loved it in equal measure. She both prayed he would find some sense of decorum in himself and learn to put on a shirt whenever they might encounter one another.

And prayed he would not.

Ever.

His chest was broad, and currently bare, a light dusting of hair over the toned, taut skin there. He took a breath, his well-defined abs shifting as he stepped to the side, as if allowing her entry into his bedchamber.

"How did you know I was out here?" She asked again, not making the move toward entering.

"I could feel the tension radiating through the door. And only you give off tension quite like that, Latika."

"Ah, yes," she said, giving a slight nod of her head. "You're very funny."

"I can *hear* you. You do not wear sensible shoes, like my sister. You wear those hard, spiky heels, and they make a very particular sound on the marble. I suppose, were I given to any great sense of shame, I would be concerned that sound can travel so freely through my bedroom door. One assumes then the sound can travel out just as well."

"A *grave* concern for you," she said, clipped. "I can only imagine."

He shrugged a broad shoulder, making all the muscles in his body shift and bunch. "It isn't really."

"It should be." She looked around the room. There were no signs of recent debauchery, at least. By that she meant, there wasn't a redhead or a blonde lying sprawled out in his bed, or anything quite like that.

However, the bed was unmade, and he had clearly just arisen from it, and likely just pulled the jeans he was wearing on.

It made her wonder if there was anything underneath.

She gritted her teeth, angry with herself without thought. "Astrid has asked me…"

"I would like you to find me a wife," he said, cutting her off and silencing her effectively.

"You… What?"

"I would like you to find me a wife. I understand that my reputation has become of some concern to Astrid. She's married, had a child, and our nation is on the brink of a great and modern future the likes of which would probably make my father rotate in his grave were he not so busy burning in hell."

"Astrid has asked me to help you reform," she finished.

"I know," he said. "And I think there's only one way to do that."

She had expected resistance. She had expected him to balk. To banter. To use excessive double entendre. She had not expected him to see her coming, to anticipate her words, and raise her.

"Why? Why are you suddenly interested in marriage?"

"I didn't say I was suddenly interested in marriage. But I do know that a fairytale is the quickest way to capture the hearts of the people. Is it not?"

"Well, judging by your sister's experience, I would say you are correct enough."

"I am not the heir. That is something that has always sat comfortably with me, but the burden that Astrid carries does not. And for my part, if I can alleviate some of what she carries, then I will do it. I can see that the simplest way will be for me to find a wife."

"A bizarre leap in logic."

"I know you don't respect me, Latika, and I have

never asked you to. Moreover, I've never behaved in a way that might invite you to. Oddly, though it may seem to you, I'm not overly concerned with your approval. But, I do wish to make Astrid happy, and I do wish to bolster the standing of my country in the world. So, you must help me find a wife."

"Is there a particular brand name you are drawn to?" she asked, her tone caustic.

"Yes," he said, not missing a beat. "I would prefer a philanthropist. I do not require that she be in mint condition, so to speak."

It took her a moment to catch his meaning. "You do not expect a virgin? How progressive of you."

"Well," he said. "As I myself am not a virgin, it seems a bit of a double standard to demand my wife come to me untouched."

She tried to keep the flush out of her face, and tried to keep her tone sharp. "You are not untouched?"

The corner of his wicked mouth turned up. "I've been touched one or two times."

"Shocking," she returned.

"I expect that you possess ample channels through which you might find a woman interested in marrying me."

The very idea of arranging marriages didn't sit very well with Latika. Not given her experience surrounding such things. Of course, Gunnar didn't know anything about her real life. Or her real identity. Fishing around in the sorts of circles that might require him to find a wife in might present a problem for her as well.

Considering she was technically in hiding.

But then, she could find ways to be discreet. Find

ways to make sure that she avoided any places that might be problematic.

Just one grim corner of Europe, and the East Coast of the United States. She imagined that Gunnar wouldn't mind her fishing around for an English debutante, rather than looking on the Upper Eastside of New York City.

"Blonde? Redheaded? Brunette? Do you have a preference?"

"None," he said.

"You don't have a type?" she pressed.

"*Female* covers it."

She fought against rolling her eyes. Instead, she made a very officious note on her clipboard. Then treated him to a smile. "A female philanthropist. Hymen not required."

"In fact, I would prefer that there were no hymen present at all," he said. "I'm not a patient man. I'd rather not have to instruct a woman on how to please me."

"Indeed," she said flatly. And she managed to hold back: *that rules me out handily then.*

As if she would ever, in a million years, with flying pigs in the sky, consider being Gunnar's bride.

He turned away from her, his broad back filling her vision. His muscles moved in very interesting ways and she attempted to study the ceiling, rather than his skin.

But it was hard, because his skin was so much more compelling.

And he began to move around the room. He opened up a dresser, pulled out a T-shirt, and shrugged it over his body.

Something about the flex of those muscles caused an answering flex between her thighs, and she did her best to ignore it.

Her emotions were so very charged in his presence, always. And it was her preference to play off the heat as anger. And to pretend that there was no other layer to it.

That there was no part of her—not even a tiny part—that wished to bite down on that insolent mouth of his.

And then bite his chest.

And then lick it.

No. No part of her at all.

She forced a smile. "Anything else?"

"No. I believe that covers it."

"Then I shall begin putting out inquiries, Your Highness. And very soon, I will have found a wife for you."

"It may also bear mentioning," he said, "That I am the owner of my own multibillion-dollar company."

Latika froze. "You... You're what?"

"Yes. I suppose it's about time that came out."

"How... How did you keep that a secret?"

"No one is looking for that bit of dirt. Honestly, it isn't dirt. Why would anyone care? My company has a name, obviously, and *my* name is buried beneath it. But the only thing anyone is ever interested in is who I'm sleeping with. Not the fact that I am the CEO of a multibillion-dollar corporation that deals in green building."

"I..."

"It's part of revamping my reputation, Latika. These things must be made public. I assume you're the person to speak to about the press release regarding that as well."

"I will take care of it," she said, blinking.

"See that you do."

Those blue eyes caught hers and held for a moment, and Latika did her best not to pay attention to the slight shift she felt in her stomach. Did her best to ignore the fact that suddenly the air felt a little bit thicker.

And she really tried not to examine what any of this new information—that he was not going into any of this kicking and screaming, that he had an endeavor that went somewhere beyond gambling and whoring—made her feel.

She was much more comfortable when she disdained Gunnar.

Anything else was unacceptable.

Prince Gunnar von Bjornland had settled into debauchery for far too long. He was at an end with it.

It had been one thing to engage in it when his father was living, and indeed it was something that he had enjoyed.

To throw in the face of his father, even as the old man attempted to sabotage Astrid. Their father was a relic of the highest order. A man who had not been able to fathom that a woman could possibly do a good job of running the country, regardless of the fact that there were many examples that proved they could, and just fine thank you.

No, his father had never gotten over the fact that his heir was a woman. And the fact that his only son had refused to take his side and engage in a coup, overthrowing his twin had been something that the old man could not accept even in the end.

Gunnar had never risen to his father's bait, and to the contrary, had taken a perverse kind of delight in behaving in every way that Astrid did not.

As his sister had lived a serious and contemplative life, dedicating herself to service, Gunnar had waged an all-out war against propriety.

He had taken every sacred tradition and broken it at least once, had taken delight in running roughshod over deeply revered customs, and in general putting Bjornland on the world stage in the context of his behavior.

He had imagined that if nothing else he would be a rather colorful footnote in history.

But of course, it had never been enough for his mind. Hence the secret business endeavor.

But now that Astrid was Queen, and now that various and sundry accusations were being thrown at him as the narrative around his country shifted, he could see that it was time for a change.

This latest debacle had only served to highlight it.

A woman had come forward alleging that he was the father of her child. And no matter that Gunnar had never seen the woman before, there had also been a seed of doubt in him. He always used protection. But condoms weren't entirely reliable, and he'd had to concede that there was a possibility the child could be his, no matter that he was always as responsible as a man could be while being indiscriminate.

The headlines had been scathing, the very fact that a paternity test had been conducted had been cause for scorn among the people.

And now the conversation had become that Astrid could not control her wayward brother. That her own brother despised every value held dear by the country. And when that had been aimed at his father, Gunnar had been happy enough.

But his entire reason for his behavior, his entire reason for being, had been to protect Astrid. Astrid was a strong woman, and always had been, but there had been a war waging beneath the surface of the polished exterior of the palace that she'd had no idea existed.

A war that Gunnar had been on the frontlines of.

He had always protected her. And if protecting his sister now demanded he behave differently, so he would.

And if it meant employing the use of his sister's delectable, and irritating, assistant, then he would do so.

Latika might be delectable, but she was also as stiff as a plank of wood and no less bland.

She was beautiful. There was no argument to be had about that.

In fact, she was uncommonly lovely, and he had always found it a strange thing that a woman of such brilliant beauty be relegated to such a *beige* sort of job.

Though, he imagined a great many people would not find being personal assistant to a queen a *beige sort of job.* But in his world it certainly was.

A woman like her should be wrapped in silk, should be in jewels.

She should spend hours soaking in perfumed baths, readying herself for a lover.

She should *not* spend hours contemplating the merit of clipboards. Though, he had a feeling that was how she spent much of her time.

Her beauty was, in the end, a terrible farce anyway. She looked like a woman built for such things, with her generous mouth and beautiful curves, but she was through and through a woman of practicality and severity.

And he did his very best not to think about how much he would like to test that severity.

He did his very best not to think about just how satisfying it would be to tease that mouth out of that firm unnatural line she kept it in, and torment her until it became a soft "O" of pleasure.

Yes, he did his best not to ponder that.

His world was changing. He would need to find a wife, and he would need to be faithful to that wife.

The very idea of such a chore set his teeth on edge. He could think of no woman at all that would amuse him for the rest of his life, and if he quit engaging in risky behaviors such as racing cars around the autobahn and jumping out of helicopters, his life would likely have a longer expectancy.

Really, this was a terrible plan, but it was the only way he could see to help Astrid.

Though she did not know it, his life had been devoted to that protection.

He would not falter now.

Marriage was, in the grand scheme of things a small price to pay. And for her he would do it. Perhaps not happily, but it would be done.

Because Gunnar von Bjornland might never be King, but he was the master of his own life. And once he set his mind to something, he would damn well see it done.

This was no exception.

CHAPTER TWO

"HERE YOU HAVE IT," Latika said, setting a stack of folders onto Gunnar's desk. "Veritable binders of women."

He looked at the stack, then back up at Latika, one elbow resting on the desk, one brow raised in an impudent manner. "I'm rather insulted you have brought me so much choice," he said.

Latika blinked. "How is that insulting?"

"I should think that the criteria for becoming my bride would be so exacting that you would have little more than a slim volume to present me with."

"I should have thought you would want choice," she said, bristling against his rather pronounced lack of gratitude.

She had gone to a lot of trouble to dig up so many eligible women, lacking in scandal and in possession of beauty.

"I haven't time to do so much reading," he said.

"Do you find it so laborious? To read profiles on women you might marry."

"I find it *boring*."

"I have here in these folders options, for a woman that you might be tasked with sleeping with for the rest of your life. How is it you find that dull?" she pressed.

"When one turns sex into homework even that can be boring."

He was *impossible*. He was impossible, and he was ridiculous, and she had half a mind to kill him where he sat. She could do it with a letter opener, a paperweight or half a dozen other items on his desk.

As solid as her friendship with Astrid was, she had a feeling that Astrid would take a dim view to Latika assassinating her brother. Just maybe. If Astrid only knew the surrounding story she might forgive her.

"Who do you think the top five are?" he asked. "Use your knowledge of me to guess who I might find the most likely five."

"Gunnar," she said, keeping her tone frosty. "If I had that kind of insight into who you are as a person… Well, I would probably throw myself off the nearest cliff."

"A test then." He folded his large hands in front of him and it didn't escape her notice they were scarred. Odd for a man of his position, she would think. "Who do *you* think my top five would be?"

Latika gritted her teeth. She would lie back and think of Bjornland. She would do her very best to remind herself she worked for the palace.

And this was service to Astrid.

And for Astrid, she could do anything. The other woman had essentially saved Latika's life. And it was something that she was not going to forget anytime soon. Or ever. She was eternally grateful for all that Astrid had done. Working with Gunnar on this marriage project was a small thing to ask.

"All right," she said, doing her best to cover up just how aggrieved she felt. "If I had to choose, I would choose not so much to please *you*, but to give maximum improvement to your reputation, and to the reputation of the country. Therefore, we can set aside your personal preferences as secondary."

He rubbed his chin, the light in his blue eyes wicked. "*Can* we?"

"Yes," she said decisively. "This marriage is for the country, after all."

"And yet, I feel that if I am to be shackled to one woman for the rest of my life, it will have to be a marriage bed that I enjoy the idea of being shackled to." His lips curved upward. "Rather, a woman not averse to being shackled to the marriage bed for my pleasure. I've never been one who enjoyed being shackled. But I have nothing against doing a bit of shackling."

Yet again, she ignored the searing heat in her body, and affected an incredibly bored expression. "Yes, yes. I and the rest of the world are aware of the fact that you are shocking, and love to engage in *edgy* sexual activity. I promise you that if a double entendre presents itself you do not have to be so obvious as to speak it."

"Oh, but I enjoy being obvious."

"Do you?" she asked. "Because I would say that the fact you own your own company was not obvious at all."

She hadn't intended to bring that up.

In fact, she had every intention of ignoring it completely in the conversation today, if only to spite him slightly. And herself. Because the fact that he was a secret mogul fascinated her. And the one thing she was eternally trying to ignore when it came to Gunnar was her fascination with him. And anything that seemed to foster further fascination she resented.

There was something about him that enticed her to act in ways she knew she should not. She didn't like it.

It made her feel like she was not above the rest of the female population of the world in any way at all. And she liked to think that she wasn't that basic.

"That's the trick," he said. "Be obvious enough over here that you can have your secrets where you choose."

"I see." She took a breath. "Well. That aside." She shuffled through the folder and plucked out one. "I would choose…these."

"Explanations," he demanded, taking the stack of folders in his hand. "Or do I have to do everything myself."

"You have done absolutely nothing for yourself since I walked in," she said.

"That isn't true. I've been breathing the entire time. I'm keeping myself alive. For which you and the rest of the world should be supremely grateful."

"I'm about to expire from gratitude," she said. "The first candidate is Hannah Whitman, an English rose. She will compliment you well. Though, your progeny will likely burst into flames in the sun."

He laughed, explosive and deep, hitting her in unexpected places.

"Well," he said. "Melanin deficit aside, she is pretty. And what attributes do you suppose she would bring to our alliance?"

"She's extremely wealthy in her own right, her family is very successful in manufacturing. She has started several charities, with a focus on educating children with special needs. She is more than willing to do the work, not simply write a check."

"I imagine that means there are many photographs of her with grateful children."

"You are correct. She is a light to all the world."

"Well, I have always thought that one's wife should be able to double as a flashlight."

"Best of all," Latika continued, "she's scandal free."

"Excellent. Because I have enough scandals for ten people. It's one thing I do not need a wife to bring to our marriage."

"Next is Lily Addington."

"Another Brit?"

"Yes. Her family owns horses."

He frowned. "That sounds like an awful lot of time spent at racetracks."

"Would you not find that enjoyable?"

"No. I prefer my gambling to take place in a casino. It's much more civilized."

"All right. Bim Attah. She is a Nigerian heiress and UN ambassador for women's rights. She has a PhD from Oxford, and has been instrumental in supplying feminine hygiene products to impoverished girls throughout the world."

He leaned back in his chair, placing his hands behind his head. "She sounds a bit overqualified, don't you think? PhD. I'm not sure I'm equal to that task."

"You have a title. I suspect that in many ways that outstrips a PhD."

"One you are born with," he pointed out. "One you must work for."

She arched a brow. "Shall I take her off the list?"

"Oh, no," he said. "I feel nothing if not entitled to things that might be too good for me. Leave her on the list."

She cycled through the rest of them quickly with Gunnar vetoing all but numbers one and three.

"Okay," she said, sighing heavily. "I will attempt to

arrange a meeting for you. Whatever you do, try not to be yourself when you meet them."

"I never am," Gunnar said. "Why, when there are so many other interesting people to choose to be?"

Latika gritted her teeth. "Why indeed."

She turned away from him, and her phone buzzed in her hand. She looked down and saw that it was an unknown number.

"Oh, don't decline the call on account of me," Gunter said. "There's no need to worry about manners in my presence."

"I wouldn't," she said, answering the phone decisively. It had nothing to do with her anyway. She worked for Astrid, and she couldn't afford to miss any kind of communication just in case.

"Hello?"

"Latika Bakshmi."

The voice was strange, low and husky, and something about the accent sent a familiar sliver of dread beneath Latika's skin.

"Yes?"

"Check your email."

The line went dead. Latika lowered the phone and stared at it, feeling like she lost herself for a full thirty seconds. She had no sense of where she was, or what she was doing.

Until she felt the intensity of Gunnar's gaze on the side of her face. She looked toward him. "What?"

"Are you all right?"

"I'm fine."

"You've gone very pale."

"No. A strange phone call. Likely a prank of some kind." She tried to force a smile. In spite of herself, she swallowed hard and guided her thumb over the email icon on her phone.

She prayed that Gunnar didn't notice the slight tremble in her hands.

She did indeed have a new email.

From an address she didn't recognize. She opened the email, it had one line of text. And a photograph.

So there you are.

And beneath those words was a picture. Zoomed in tightly and cropped close. Latika could just see the edge of Astrid's dress, and that gave her an indication of the event.

The wedding.

Astrid and Mauro's wedding. Latika had been standing just behind the Queen, and she had been sure that she was not in any sort of limelight position. She had been with Astrid for nearly four years and never had been.

But they had found her. Finally.

She swallowed hard, fear like lead in her stomach.

The worst part was, it hadn't been her parents who had found her. She was sure of that. Because while her parents would have happily hauled her away from her newfound life, they wouldn't engage in this level of theatrics. That she knew.

They would still cling to the idea that this was all for her own good, for their own good as well, but also for hers. They would lie to her, lie to themselves, all the while using soft, soothing voices and telling her to think of the future.

No, this kind of threatening language was definitely

the work of the man who was supposed to be her husband by now.

The man she had run away from.

The man she would rather die than find herself joined to.

Latika took a breath and put her hands down, holding her phone closely to her thigh.

"What is it?" Gunnar asked.

"Nothing," she said. "I will make the necessary inquiries, and make arrangements for you to meet these women. In fact, I think we will organize a ball."

"A ball?"

"Yes. For all the eligible ladies in the file."

"I said that I'm only interested in these two."

"But why limit your options, Your Highness. You're correct. The chemistry that you may feel with one of them is important to explore. Allow me to take care of it. I will handle everything."

Her mind was spinning as she walked out of Gunnar's office. On the one hand, creating such a spectacle around the country at this time was possibly unwise. But on the other hand… Well, on the other hand an event like this would necessitate an increase in security. And with so many eyes on the country, she imagined that Ragnar would be loath to attempt to take her now.

No, he preferred to do things secretly. In the dark of night, essentially.

His position as Norwegian nobility mattered far too much for him to go and create bad blood between himself and the Royals in Bjornland.

And in truth, Latika had counted on that. Always. When she had first come to Astrid for the job, it had been on her mind. The fact that Bjornland was politically involved with Norway, and that it would put Ragnar in a bad position should he cross the Queen, had mattered to her.

Because she needed protection.

The palace guards would provide it. The increased attention would provide it. She had to believe that.

The alternative was far too awful to consider.

CHAPTER THREE

THE ENSUING WEEK was a whirlwind. At least, it looked as though it were one for Latika.

Gunnar did nothing but sit back and enjoy the show.

Over breakfast one morning, Astrid commented on it. "I don't think I've ever seen her work so hard at anything. And that's saying quite a bit."

"Yes, she has taken control of the task admirably," he said, not rising to his sister's bait. Because he knew there was bait. Even if he wasn't sure what the hook buried in said bait was meant to drag him toward.

"Are you assisting her at all?" Astrid asked.

"Do *you* assist her in the planning of parties?"

Astrid gave him an icy look. "She is *my* assistant."

At that moment, Astrid's husband came into the room holding Gunnar's nephew. It had taken Gunnar a time to accept his brother-in-law. He had not trusted the man at first, but then, given the way that his sister had met him, Gunnar felt he could hardly be blamed.

Astrid had engaged in subterfuge, essentially tricking Mauro into getting her pregnant. And when he had discovered the ruse, Mauro had been decisive in his action. He had demanded that Astrid marry him, and that, was what Gunnar had taken exception to.

The man was common born, and it wasn't as if Gunnar was any sort of snob, but he had grave concerns about anyone seeking to use his sister. As it had turned out, his feelings for Astrid had been genuine and their marriage had become a very happy one.

But, Gunnar was still getting used to the situation.

"That's different," Astrid said, rising from her seat and crossing the room, giving Mauro a kiss on the cheek before taking her son into her arms. "You should be helping her. Since she is helping you clean up your mess."

For Astrid.

He wasn't going to say that. He didn't care what anyone thought of him. And were it not for his sister, he would happily go on not caring.

"I'm sorry, what exactly did you want me to do?" he asked. "Ensure that the punch is spiked?"

"I don't know, something that wouldn't send my assistant to an early grave. Since I am quite attached to her."

"Yes," he said. "Something that I'm not sure I understand. You seem more fond of her than you are of me at times. And yet, for all I can tell, Latika seems to lack a sense of fun, or humor."

"That's a phenomenon that only presents itself in your presence, Gunnar. I find her amusing and delightful." His sister's gaze was glued to him. "Perhaps it's just you."

"Everybody likes me."

"Everyone thinks you can do something for them. That's different. I don't think Latika cares one way or the other whether or not you can do something for her."

That wasn't true. Everyone was an opportunist. And

everyone would use a person if the need was great enough. He'd learned that early, and he'd learned it well.

Nothing could insulate you when someone decided to use you as a tool. Not even family. Not even blood.

"She works for you. If she needs a favor... You're the one she'll go to," he pointed out.

"Are you implying she doesn't actually *like* me?"

"Did you not just imply that none of my friends actually like me?"

"Are either of you going to threaten to have the guards shoot the other this time?" Mauro asked, his brother-in-law's expression one of amusement.

"Probably not," Astrid said.

"The two of you make me so sad that I was an only child," Mauro said.

"I can see where you would be jealous," Astrid responded serenely.

They settled in to eat breakfast then, and Gunnar was bemused by the domesticity before him. It was difficult to imagine himself settling into such a life.

And yet, he didn't think it would make him entirely miserable. Of course, he would never feel for his wife the way that Mauro and Astrid seemed to feel for each other.

And there would be no children in his marriage.

The line was guaranteed to continue without his help, and he was not the heir. Therefore the task wasn't his.

After the childhood he'd endured, he had no interest in exploring the relationship between a parent and child again. Even from the opposite side.

The door opened, and Latika entered, her black hair swept back into a twist, her makeup sedate. And yet, she glowed. He ignored the tightness that he felt in his stomach. In his groin.

"I do hope I'm not interrupting," she said. "Queen Astrid, we have an appointment with your stylist. We must ensure that you are appropriately outfitted for the ball."

"What about me?" Gunnar asked.

"You will wear a black suit," Latika said, each word crisp.

She was like a tart apple. Then he desperately wanted to take a bite of her.

It was a shame. For with this new endeavor now before him, he never would.

For years now, his dearest fantasy had been getting down on his knees before his sister's prim assistant, pushing one of her tight pencil skirts up around her hips and draping her legs over his shoulder, her back against the wall, as he licked his way into her center.

As if she sensed his thoughts, her gaze landed on his, locked there. She looked startled, like a deer caught in the headlights.

"It seems to me that you are avoiding having to dress me," he said.

"I'm not avoiding anything," she said. "Believe me, Gunnar, if you required dressing, I would accommodate. I'm sorry if that wounds your fragile masculinity in any way."

"Good to know," he said.

On a tightlipped smile, Latika turned and walked out of the room.

Astrid fixed her cold gaze on him. "Can you not deliberately poke at her with a stick?"

"I'm not poking her."

"You're a pain in the ass. She's been through enough without you harping on her constantly. Be a decent human being."

"That is, dear sister, the point of all of this."

If he could not fashion himself into a decent human in the realest sense, he would make himself look like one.

In his world, facade was better than reality anyway.

Two hours after the encounter with Gunnar in the dining room had left Latika trembling and feeling hollowed out, she found herself standing in Astrid's chamber while her friend tried on a myriad of dresses.

"It seems strange," Astrid said, currently admiring a white gown with delicate silver beading that clung to her curves. "To draw attention to myself on what should be a ball in my brother's honor."

"Yes," Latika said. "I can see that. But you know, it is about improving the way people look at all of Bjornland. We have essentially put out a call to all the eligible ladies of the world that Prince Gunnar is looking to settle down. The media attention alone demands that you shine above all else. Especially all those eligible ladies. It won't do to have anyone in attendance be more beautiful than the Queen."

Astrid laughed. "I imagine there will be a great many women there who are more beautiful. My brother attracts rare beauties like honey attracts bees."

"Yes," Latika said. "Pity he is not actually sweet."

"I don't think anyone would find him half so compelling if he were."

Compelling.

That was an appropriate word for the man.

Of course, there were other words too. None of them fit for polite company.

"I think this color washes me out," Astrid said. She looked over at the rack that was entirely filled with gowns. "And that orange would be hideous on me. It would look lovely on you."

She gestured to a gown with a long bodice and a full, sheer skirt that gathered at the side, with a close fitted lining beneath. It was orange, with shimmering gold geometric detail over the top of it.

And, Latika *knew* she would look good in it.

But, she needed stay in the background. Desperately.

"I think I will opt for something black," she said decisively.

"Well," Astrid said. "I will not. I would look like a ghost."

Astrid sighed and then looked over at Latika thoughtfully. "Are you all right?"

"I'm fine," Latika said.

"You don't look fine. In fact, you seem very tense. And not simply because you're planning a party. Usually, you enjoy that."

"Well, it's just Gunnar. You know he and I don't exactly see eye to eye. But it's normal. Nothing out of the ordinary." Except the threats to her safety. But she was choosing to handle that herself.

Astrid blinked. "Yes. I do know that the two of you get on like angry ants trapped in a jar. I also don't think that's the real problem."

"Why?" Latika asked.

"Because I know you. Because we're friends. Latika, don't you trust me?"

Latika shifted uncomfortably. "Of course I do."

"Are you upset about Gunnar getting married?"

Latika sputtered. "What?"

"I'm not a fool," Astrid said. "I know that he irritates you, but I also know that there is something underneath that. I can never tell if the two of you are going to start yelling at each other, or start tearing each other's clothes off."

Latika stiffened, her face getting hot. The fact that Astrid had noticed that she carried some sort of shameful…fascination with Gunnar was truly alarming. It was somewhat refreshing to be able to be alarmed about something other than the email she'd received a few days ago, though, she would not have chosen this. "I can honestly say that I am not upset about Gunnar choosing to get married."

"Then what is it? Please don't tell me it's to do with your parents."

Latika sighed. "Not as such."

"It's related to that, though."

"I… I have reason to believe that my former fiancé knows where I am."

"Latika, that's terrible. You should have told me immediately. I will do whatever I have to, to protect you."

"And I will do whatever I need to, to protect *you*. You don't need to worry about me, or the issues that I'm having. The scandals in my life were never meant to touch you."

"That's not how friendship works," Astrid said. "Yes, you have been an employee, but more than that. And you know it. You are the single best friend I've ever had. It's because of you that I found my husband."

"In fairness," Latika said, "it was highly unlikely any of that would work, and I feel it was only a stroke of incredible luck that saw it all come together. Or fate, perhaps. But either way, I cannot take credit. And had everything gone awry, I would have been responsible for your most disastrous decision ever. We could have damaged the whole of the country over a one-night stand."

"But it was meant to be," Astrid said. "And you trusted me. You trusted me when I said I needed your help, and believe me, the people in my life who have trusted me, who have taken me at my word, have been in short supply. For the most part, people have doubted I know my own mind because I am a woman. Really, only you and Gunnar, and my mother, ever treated me as though I had the head on my shoulders required to run a country. Or, to make any decisions on my own."

"Yes," Latika said. "Well."

It was one of the difficult things about Gunnar. He had always been incredibly supportive of his sister. And though he had been angry over the incident with Mauro, and Latika colluding with Astrid to sneak her into his club so that she might engage his services in the making of an heir, in many ways, Latika couldn't blame him. And indeed, would possibly respect him less if he'd had no issue with it whatsoever.

Latika had helped Astrid accomplish that for her own reasons, but it certainly wasn't in the interest of her finding love with Mauro. No. It was only that she understood what it was like to feel that you had no power in your own life.

An ancient law written into the code of the land of Bjornland had stated that the Queen could declare herself the sole parent of her issue. With that goal in mind, Astrid had set out to get pregnant by the most disreputable man on the planet, thinking he would want nothing to do with the child. Of course, he had. And Astrid had not ended up with a child, and no man, but with a husband. One that she loved very dearly. Nothing had gone quite as they planned, but in many ways, it had gone better.

Latika had never seen Astrid so happy.

And that—she had concluded—was what happened when people were allowed to live. To make their own choices.

To make their own *mistakes*.

Sometimes even a mistake—in the end—was perfectly all right because it led you to where you had always been meant to be.

But choice, that was what Latika wanted. Eventually. A life of her choosing, with a man of her choosing.

She wanted children.

Watching Astrid with Mauro all those desires had only become more pronounced.

She was tired of surviving.

And with Ragnar coming after her those dreams seemed farther away than ever. Dreams other people took for granted.

"What can I do to protect you?" Astrid said. "Your problems are mine. Because we are friends."

"Honestly, this ball is going to offer me a modicum of protection I would not have access to if it weren't for my position here. We will, of course have to increase security. Seeing as we are inviting every eligible woman in the world to come and have a chance with Gunnar. And those who haven't met him will surely jump at the opportunity."

Astrid erupted into a peal of laughter. "You do protest too much, Latika."

"Perhaps my protestations are honest," she said.

"You find my brother attractive. Whether you want to admit it or not."

"A spider can be beautiful in its web," Latika said. "But that doesn't mean I want it on my skin."

Astrid shook her head. "But see, that's where you have him wrong. He's not a spider. Any more than you're a fly. A predator, possibly. But maybe more like the wolves we have here in the mountains. Deadly if necessary, surely. But more than willing to put everything on the line to protect his pack. Gunnar is a true alpha. Leader and protector."

"Perhaps that's the problem," Latika said. "It is difficult for two alphas to get involved."

"That would be the story of my marriage," Astrid said. "But what Mauro and I have learned is that sometimes it can be quite pleasurable to let the other take the lead."

"Yes, well." Latika firmed her lips into a straight line. "I will take the lead by finding some other woman for Gunnar to harass."

"Are you sure you don't want to wear this?" Astrid asked, gesturing to the orange gown again.

"No," Latika returned. "I am not one of the women vying for your brother's attention, and I will not dress like one. It would have to be a moment of true crisis in order for me to turn to him."

"Well, let us hope we had don't have any crises ahead of us."

CHAPTER FOUR

THE EVENING OF the ball, everything was going according to plan. Latika could find no fault with anything.

And she ignored the orange and gold gown that Astrid had sent up for her, in favor of a long, formfitting black dress and simple gold accessories. She would look appropriate, and she would *blend*.

And that was the idea.

She bustled around, making sure that everything was in place, pacing the length of the ornate ballroom, examining it from the gilt-edged ceilings, all the way down to the marble floors.

The massive, golden chandelier was lit, and it was like a sun burning brightly at the center of the room. Perfect. Gleaming and lovely. And in the next twenty minutes the ball would be full of fluttering flowers, all vying for Gunnar's attention.

She heard footsteps on the marble floor, and turned.

And there he was.

He was devastating in that custom cut black suit, the one she had dismissed with a wave of her hand, saying that men needn't be so concerned with such things.

There was nothing *plain* about Gunnar in a black

suit. He was a weapon against all good sense, his broad
shoulders waging war on every prudent thought.

His hair was still overlong, brushed away from his
face, his beard just a bit unkempt.

And it put her in the mind of a Norse marauder, and
she found that however she tried, she could not dislike
the image.

And for the first time, a strange pain hollowed out
her stomach.

Another woman would dance in his arms tonight.
Another woman would dance with him from tonight,
possibly into forever.

And she would never know what it was like to be
held by those strong arms.

She clenched her teeth. That was an empty fantasy,
driven by hormones. And she was not a slave to her
hormones. She was a woman who never had such a luxury. She had been driven by the need to survive. By the
need to press forward, always, and make for herself a
life that she could not only stand, but that she enjoyed.

She had found a way to live.

It might not be her ideal life, yet. But it was wonderful.

And she was only ever proud of herself for that fact.

Gunnar served no purpose. Attraction to Gunnar
served no purpose.

She did not even like the man.

"You have done a spectacular job," he said, and she
ignored the slight thrill of pleasure that went through
her midsection.

"Thank you," she said.

"Soon, I will be like a steak put out before the dogs."

The wicked glint in his eye bade her stomach turn over. She ignored the sensation.

"You will find there are no dogs here. Only a wolf," she said, harking back to Astrid's earlier words.

He grinned, and Latika thought it was decidedly wolfish. "Perhaps."

"Sheep," Latika said. "Sheep going before a wolf."

"Very evocative. Does that make you Little Red Riding Hood in this fairytale of a metaphor? Because I must tell you, I feel my mouth is all the better to eat you with."

And that was when she realized, he was not simply engaging in empty banter. No, there was a gleam in his blue eyes that spoke of intent. But there was no point to him making sexual promises toward her. Not when tonight, of all nights, moved any possibility of something happening between them out of reach.

She ignored the jolt of irritation that she felt over that. The intense regret.

Every time he had ever traded barbs with her she had assumed it was simply who he was, what he did.

She had never once thought that he might... That he might actually want her.

"I am not anyone's version of a fairytale. And you would find, that I bite back."

He moved closer to her, and a thrill shot down her spine. "Pity for you, that what you intended as a threat only sounds like a promise to me. I like a woman who gives as good as she gets."

"Then I suggest you find one here in the room full of them."

"I doubt there will be one sharp as you."

"The trade-offs you make for respectability," she said.

She turned away from him and began to busy herself with details that did not need her attention.

"Are you not respectable?"

"That depends, I suppose," she said, "on your definition of respectability."

Those blue eyes regarded her with open interest. "Someday, I should like to find out."

She locked her teeth together. So tight her jaw ached. "Oh, but there is no someday. For you are getting married. And we all know your life will end as we know it."

"A tragedy," he said.

"Well," she said, brushing her hands down the front of her dress. "It's time to bring in the staff. And then it will be time to open up the doors. I suggest you get in position."

He arched a brow, a wicked smile curving his lips. "Missionary? Did you have something else in mind," he said.

Latika ignored the sharp shock of pleasure that shot straight down through her core. It was wrong for them to talk like this—worse to be talking like this tonight. Though in some ways, it pushed it further out of the realm of possibility than ever. Which made it…almost less wrong maybe? Or less dangerous.

"You will look a bit silly in missionary position on your own," she shot back, unwilling to let him see that he had affected her.

"I suppose that depends on who you ask."

The doors opened then, and the staff began to filter inside. Latika managed to busy herself and soon her interaction with Gunnar was forgotten. She had work to do. It distracted her, both from the strange sensation she felt whenever she was around the man, and from the underlying sense of fear she'd been feeling ever since she received that email.

The many, many palace guards in attendance made her feel safe.

No one would do anything to her while she was here.

She repeated all those things to herself as she made sure the food was in place, as she made sure all was well. And then, went back to the antechamber to ensure that everything was ready for Astrid to make her appearance.

Several guests arrived before the Queen was to be seated. And Latika had the task of making sure that Astrid's entrance went smoothly, and according to plan.

Astrid and Mauro looked beautiful, the pair of them absolute perfection. Astrid had ended up choosing a deep emerald gown, and her husband was in a black suit. Mauro was a handsome man. There was no denying it. Tall, dark and Mediterranean, with wicked eyes and a mouth that looked like it was made for sin.

And yet, it was no particular sin that called to Latika. No, there was something about the cold, wild beauty that Gunnar possessed that seemed to ignite thoughts of sin.

Sin that sorely tempted her.

She put her head down, resolutely making her way through the ballroom, now filled with women that were bedecked as tropical birds, fluttering about in bright colors.

She knew that Gunnar had expressed a preference for two women in particular, but the guests did not. And every one woman—single or not—had dressed to impress him.

Latika cued everyone to Astrid and Mauro's entrance, and the royal couple alit, walking through the crowd and taking their positions in their honored seats.

It was all going so smoothly Latika wanted to celebrate. That was the thing. She might not have a husband or children yet. She might not be fully living the life of her choice, but she was living well.

She'd been seen by her parents as a bargaining chip. Her only value had been how she could marry. And here she was, operating in a very stressful and important career.

And she did it well.

She allowed that to buoy her mood. To take away the sour feelings that had begun to roil in her stomach earlier.

With them settled, Latika felt the need to check on the kitchen. She turned and slipped out a side entrance, heading down the hall. And what she saw there made her stomach twist. It was him.

Ragnar.

He didn't have the decency to be hideous. No, instead he was a severe looking older man with salt-and-pepper hair and a neat beard. He was handsome. And a great many women—regardless of their age—would have been thrilled with his attentions. But Latika knew how cruel he could be. And she knew that a life with him would be equal to misery.

The fact that he had come after her after all this time, likely less out of an attraction for her specifically, and more because he wished her harm, sent fear rattling through her.

"My dear, Latika," he said. "It has been quite some time."

"Not accidentally," she said, stopping in her tracks

and beginning to edge back toward the ballroom. There was security there. And she would be able to call for help.

"Do not think I'm so foolish as to try and take you from the palace. I simply wanted you to know how close I am. If you try to leave the country, my agents will intercept you. And I know you are here. Ultimately, as long as I can reach you, you are not safe. I will have you brought back to Norway, and married to me before you could ever protest."

"And why would I marry you?" She asked, fighting to keep her composure.

He liked fear. He liked to cause pain.

She would allow him to see neither in her.

"Because you will find the alternatives so unpleasant. You have made for yourself a little problem here. You thought that by making yourself invisible you would become invisible to me, but you are not just invisible to me, but the whole world. And that is where you have failed yourself, my darling girl. Because when I take you, I will be able to hide you. Your Queen may miss you, but how will she mobilize forces beyond the borders of her country? The public outcry will never be sufficient enough."

The words settled down to her bones, the truth of them making her feel fear. Real and heavy.

He continued. "I have you between a rock wall and me. And you know that it is true. For now... I will be here all night."

"I can have you removed," she said, craning her neck.

"I have done nothing," he said. "And my removal would create an international incident. As you well know. I know you do not wish for an incident. You are too smart of a girl for something like that." She swallowed hard, and turned and fled, running back into the ballroom, shutting the door behind her, pressing her hand to her chest.

And she saw Gunnar. At the center of the room dancing with a woman. The brilliant Nigerian activist.

And suddenly, she had an idea.

Times were desperate. And so was she.

She made her way across the ballroom, heading toward the opposite door she had just come in. A door that would take her away from Ragnar.

With purpose, Latika left the ballroom, and headed toward her room.

Though she didn't know it at the time, Astrid had given her an escape. And Latika knew well enough to take it.

Gunnar was dancing with his third potential bride of the night when a hush fell over the ballroom. He turned, following the gazes of everyone in the room. And there he saw her. Standing at the entrance to the ballroom, dressed in orange and gold, her black hair a glossy wave over one side of her shoulder.

Latika.

She did not look like an assistant. She looked like a princess.

And when she began to descend the stairs, the crowd parted for her as if she was. And then she looked at him. Deliberately. Intentionally.

And a fire ignited in his gut.

He had no idea what game she was playing. He had made it plain earlier that he was attracted to her, because he had never been the sort of man to be coy about such things.

She looked completely different than she had earlier. Though, she had still been delectable in the slinky black dress she'd been wearing, it was the sort of dress designed to make her blend in. And had she been a different woman, it might have been successful. For him, Latika would never blend in.

His greatest concern in life at this moment was that she would go on always as an unanswered need.

And he was not a man who understood denial. Not in his adult life. When he'd escaped his father's power, when it had become clear to the man that Gunnar could not be manipulated, and when it would have taken the involvement of palace guards to continue his grand experiments on Gunnar, Gunnar had taken the chance to escape into a world of sensual pleasures.

Food. Drink. Women.

Luxurious surroundings.

Most of his time spent in warm climates rather than the harsh chill of Bjornland.

He had forgotten denial. He had forgotten need.

Until her.

And while he had no moral qualms about taking Latika to his bed between now and his wedding, he did feel that perhaps the ball where he was supposed to meet his future wife was perhaps not the ideal venue for such an encounter to begin. But Latika didn't seem to agree.

She crossed the room, heading straight toward him, the expression on her face one of seductive intensity.

He wanted her. And he had, ever since she had come into his sister's employ. Every time they had sparred, it had only increased his desire for her.

And now, she paraded herself before him. As if she thought he would not be able to take action here. As if she thought he would be leashed.

"If you would excuse me," he said to his partner, a woman whose name he could no longer recall.

He stepped away from her, making his way toward Latika. And much to his shock, she increased her pace and nearly flung herself into his arms. "I would be delighted to dance with you," she said.

"What are you doing?" he murmured.

"I am sorry," she said. "You have no idea how much. But I need you. Desperately. And I think that I will not harm your objective. I think that I will further your cause."

"Do you?" he asked, keeping his voice low.

"I need you to marry me," she said. "And I need you to announce it now."

"Latika…"

And then, she did something truly shocking. She launched herself forward, and captured his mouth with her own.

Gunnar was a difficult man to surprise, indeed, until this moment he would have said it was impossible.

People were boring in their predictability.

And up until this point, Latika had been scarcely different.

She had bantered with him. She had brought their exchanges of wit to the edge of propriety, but she had never crossed it. And while he found her enjoyable, she had never truly shocked him.

But in this moment, she turned the whole ballroom— maybe the world—on its head.

There was something desperate in her kiss, and he

responded to it. He wrapped his arm around her waist, pressing her tightly against his body, forgetting they had an audience. Because what else mattered when he was finally tasting this woman that had vexed him for years.

He took control of the kiss, tightening his hold on her and angling his head, taking advantage of her surprise, of her slightly parted lips, and slipping his tongue between them.

She gasped, and he took it deeper.

And only then did he fully realize that while he might have ensnared her at this very moment, she had caught him in her trap.

"Everyone has seen," she said. "If you were to reverse course now, no one would believe you. You have clearly staked your claim on me."

"Minx," he said. "Was this your game all along?"

"I promise you it was not."

"Does my sister know that you are little more than a fortune hunter?"

"Your sister knows the truth."

He looked over at Astrid, who was seated in her throne still, watching what was taking place before her with a surprising amount of equanimity. If Astrid suspected that Latika was trying to snare him as a fortune hunter in some way, he knew that she would be on her feet.

That she would have crossed the room, making her way to him, and to Latika, demanding that the farce be ended.

But she was not. Instead, she was sitting and watching. Waiting. Clearly.

"You must say that you'll marry me," she said. "Because if you do not, there is another man here. And he is going to take me away. Not from here, but if I ever set foot outside the palace, he has promised that he will take me. If I ever leave the safety of your land. And he said… He said that my anonymity is what has cursed me, and he is not wrong. If I were to go missing, no one would know. No one would care. But if I was your wife… Gunnar, if I was your wife not only would I improve your standing in the world, but you would save me from this man. If I was your wife, I could hardly go missing without notice. Then he could not force me to marry him. I need you to protect me."

On this, Gunnar did not need a moment to think. They could work out the details later, and they would, but if what Latika said was true, she needed protection. And it was no matter to him which woman in this room he married. It might as well be the one who needed help. It might as well be the one who lit his body on fire.

"Very well," he said. "You have yourself a fiancé." He took her hand and led her over to where Astrid sat. Latika, for her part, was ashen at his side, and did not look the part of blushing bride at all. She was going to have to work on that.

"I have an announcement for you to make," he said to his sister. "It seems that I did not have to look far and wide to find my bride, as she was here the entire time."

Astrid's gaze shot to Latika. "Are you in danger?"

"I will be. If measures are not taken."

"Hello," Gunnar said. "I am the measures being taken. I assume you know about this?"

"Yes," Astrid said.

"We will speak later," he said to his sister. "For now, just make the announcement."

"I think, it's time for you to make your own."

Gunnar turned toward the crowd of people. He was not a stranger to being the center of attention, and in fact, in many venues had courted it. But never here in Astrid's domain. He had been very careful about that fact. That he never assume too much authority in his sister's presence.

Mostly, because it had angered their father.

But he was certain. Certain in this decision, whatever the eventual outcome would be.

There was no other logical choice.

"Thank you all for coming tonight. It is with great pleasure that I am able to announce that I have decided to marry. Especially in a room full of such suitable people. I will marry Latika Bakshmi in two weeks' time. You have my permission to spread the news far and wide, and to publish photographs everywhere. After all, you do know I like the show."

And with that, he grabbed Latika, and pulled her close, kissing her fiercely on the mouth. He might be aiming for a kind of propriety, but he would never be tame.

And that was something Latika would learn. He would help her, but he would never belong to her.

For he belonged to no one.

Not to Bjornland.

Not to his father.

What he did, he did because he *chose* to do it.

He had not gotten where he was by being weak.

He was unable to be brainwashed. Either by verbal suggestion or physical torture.

He'd proved that.

And he'd hidden it.

Because the only other alternative was for Astrid to

know just how desperate their father had been to have her ousted.

And he would never do that to her either.

The only line his father had was that of assassinating his own daughter.

But it had been a thin line.

He had certainly been willing to allow Gunnar to do it if he wanted to.

But Gunnar was strong.

And Gunnar protected what was his.

Now, it seemed that Latika Bakshmi was his, and he would protect her to the end.

On that he was resolved.

CHAPTER FIVE

LATIKA LOOKED TOWARD the back of the room and saw Ragnar, watching the proceedings. For a moment, she wondered what he might do. If he would pull out a weapon and assassinate her there on the spot. But then, her saving grace was the fact that he would never want his name overly sullied. And, that he would not want any physical harm to come to him. It was the biggest reason he would never make a move here. She knew that.

He cared mostly for his own self-preservation, and thanks to that predictability she was insured some level of physical safety.

He was a madman. And he was, in her opinion, nothing less than evil. But he cared for his own skin. For his own money.

And he would do nothing to compromise those things.

And so he simply stood, rendered impotent by the fact that Latika had allied herself with the most powerful man in the room.

That she was now visible.

And that if anything were to happen to her it would create something larger than an international incident.

It would create a wave of global concern.

Because while Gunnar was something of a scorned figure, particularly in his homeland, the world found the Playboy Prince to be captivating and compelling.

He was handsome, and he was roguish, and that was something that won out over respectable every single time.

If you were a man.

Well, thankfully for he was. Because as such, she had been able to use him as her salvation. But she could not escape the feeling that she had jumped from the frying pan and into the fire in many ways.

Although, at least, Gunnar would never harm her. But marriage was marriage. And it was entirely possible that she had gone from one life sentence to another.

You could not just throw yourself onto the altar of marrying a prince and expect that divorce would come easily.

It was possible, certainly. But it would not help Gunnar's reputation. It would not help Astrid's.

Standing there in front of this crowd of people with their eyes on her, putting herself in the exact opposite position to the one she had been attempting to avoid for the past several years, she felt as defeated as she did triumphant.

She had no idea what she was going to do. Not now that she had made herself so vulnerable. Not now that she had cast herself from one jail cell to another.

At least the jail keeper of this one was good-looking.

That was a shameful thought. She despised herself for it.

And even as she did, the enormity of what she had done crashed down around her. Would Gunnar expect that their marriage be real? Would he expect them to have children?

For she would have to marry him. And legally. To be absolutely certain that Ragnar would not simply be able to kidnap her and force her into marriage some other way.

She had to be legally precluded from marriage.

And still, that felt so defeating.

Because she had done all that she could to avoid being in an arranged marriage, and yet, she had gone and arranged one for herself.

Better the devil of your choosing.

Perhaps.

Her lips still burned from Gunnar's kiss. And from the kiss she'd given him earlier.

She had never kissed a man before.

And now she had. Now she had, and in two weeks, was possibly going to be sharing his bed.

And the idea didn't horrify her.

Perhaps there was another solution. Perhaps there was, and you didn't want to. Perhaps it was because you wanted him.

She ignored that voice and attempted to smile.

"Now," Gunnar said quietly to Astrid. "If you'll excuse me. I have to celebrate my engagement with my future bride. In private."

And with that, he looped his arm around her waist and began to walk her toward the door. Once they were out in the corridor, he turned to her. "Not here," she said.

"Then where, Latika? As this is your three-ring circus."

"Your bedroom," she said. "It is protected, and it is private."

"Or are you simply eager to get on with the wedding night? Because I can tell you, there are certain things I'm quite prepared to discuss naked."

"Let us go," she said.

She was trembling as they made their way down the corridor, Gunnar's hand still resting low on her back. And once they arrived in the chamber and he closed the door behind them, he turned to look at her, something cold and vicious in those icy eyes.

"Tell me honestly," he said. "Did you plan this?"

"I told you I didn't. I can take you back to the ballroom and show you the man that I'm running from. Ragnar Stevenson."

Gunnar's lip curled. "I know who he is. He has a... reputation. He has certain sexual interests that I don't approve of. There is little in this world I find distasteful or that I haven't participated in. My line, is consent, and that line is hard. He doesn't seem overly concerned with it."

"Don't you think I know? I heard all about it. I know how much he enjoys pain. Not the kind that both parties agree to enjoy together. He would much prefer to inflict it on women who do not enjoy it."

"How is it that you ended up on his radar?"

"My parents. My parents are very wealthy. They move in elite circles in America. And they wanted his nobility. His connections to Europe. The minute I found out my parents had promised me to a stranger I did as much digging around as I could. In the end it was a friend of mine's father who told me everything. He said I needed to know, and I needed to run. I tried to talk to my parents first. But they didn't believe me when I told them… They didn't believe me. They thought that

I was simply trying to get out of them choosing my husband, something I had always been trying to get out of. They said that I would not have been happy with any of their choices. My friend's father, he encouraged them to sweep my disappearance under the rug. Otherwise he…he threatened to expose them as mercenary enough to marry me to a monster."

"So they did not believe you," he said. "Even when you made it clear that their choice of husband was a sociopath. And they didn't believe your friend's father, yet they swept your disappearance under the rug when threatened with their forcing to wed being exposed?"

"That's the size of it," she said stiffly.

"Where did they tell people you'd gone?"

She rolled her eyes. "To India. To find myself. They couldn't very well tell everyone I'd gone into hiding to lose them."

"How did you find Astrid?"

"She had put out inquiries in my circle about hiring a personal assistant. Of course, a queen does not advertise in the paper. But it made the rounds on the Upper Eastside, and I found out about it. I decided that it would be a fantastic place for me to seek shelter in. I knew a great deal about putting together functions. I had a great many contacts. And I had experience organizing a variety of different events, and schedules. I knew that I could do the job, and whatever I couldn't do I would learn. Because it's really quite amazing what necessity will do for you."

"So Astrid hired you, and did not inquire about your identity?"

Latika shook her head. "I told your sister. I didn't feel right about coming here for shelter without making it very clear that I was running. It wouldn't have been fair."

Some tension drained from his body. "So you have been honest?"

"Yes. Only Astrid knew the truth. But I felt that as long as Astrid *did* know it was fair."

"I can't fault you for that."

"What is it you expect?" Latika asked. As if this had been his idea. As if he were the one who'd flung himself across the ballroom and into her arms. It wasn't fair and she knew it. But she felt slightly helpless just now, and it pained her to feel this way.

"I expect for this to be a marriage," he said. "Because there is little else that will keep him away from you."

"I know," she said, muted. "I did already think that through. An engagement would keep him at bay, and it would certainly give me more visibility. But, when we broke off the relationship I am certain that I would come out looking like the villain."

He chuckled. "How would you come across looking like a villain after the loss of an engagement to a Playboy Prince?"

"There's a very particular appendage you have that makes you much easier to forgive in the eyes of the public."

"True," he said. "I won't pretend that I don't know what you're talking about. Being Astrid's twin has not allowed for me to ignore gender disparity. She has behaved above reproach almost all the years of her life. And still, her ability to rule the country has been questioned, time and time again. I am the one whose competence should be questioned. And regularly. I have never once given the impression that I was overly competent or stable. I am. But I have never demonstrated. Astrid on the other hand has spent a lifetime devoted to Bjornland, and to cultivating a good reputation and yet...it never seems to be enough. It certainly wasn't ever enough for my father, who thought that I would be the superior choice to be on the throne by simple virtue of the fact that I have a penis."

"It is unfair," she said. "But it is true. Additionally, there would be no point in trying to cast you as the villain. The entire point of this ball, the entire point of you getting married in the first place was to improve your reputation. Should we throw up a barrier by deciding to start a rumor that you were unfaithful to me... And infidelity is the only way I could possibly see me coming out the victor... No. I won't do it. I won't do it to Astrid."

"And as you said already, it opens you up to vulnerability. No, legal marriage is likely the only thing that will keep him at bay. And a promise."

"What?"

"We will offer him something. Some sort of diplomatic prize. If he is to set foot in Bjornland again, he will find himself in a jail cell. The fact of the matter is, I have spent a great deal of time running in the circles that he has enjoyed. And I have heard many allegations from women about his behavior. Allegations themselves may not hold up in court, but we have the luxury here in this country of bypassing due process provided the crown sees fit to arrest someone."

"Could you really do that?"

"I could. It would create an incident. Likely a scandal the world over. But, I think that he is conscious enough of his own desire to stay out of prison that it will keep him well away from the borders of this country. Should he set foot over, should he show up in our immigration records, I will have him dealt with. But, that only protects you here. Outside of this place, it would not offer you protection. Only notoriety in marriage would. On that score, he was correct. But he was stupid to tell you. Stupid to think that you, a woman who has been in hiding to escape him for years, would not act in a way that was absolutely necessary to ensure your safety. Clearly, he underestimated you."

"Clearly," Latika agreed. "He underestimates women."

"Likely."

"Can we really have this done in two weeks?" she asked.

"We would be foolish not to. As you said. We must neutralize the threat. Legally tying you to another man, and embroiling you in a media circus so that everyone in the entire world knows your face… It is the easiest way to keep you safe. You must either be invisible or visible to all. And as you have lost your invisibility…"

"How long will the marriage last?" she asked.

"I am sorry, darling, but marriage is forever. At least, from my view it must be."

"But I…"

"If you thought that you could use me as a temporary solution, I'm afraid that you were mistaken. You're very clever, throwing yourself at my mercy and crying sanctuary. But we are a royal family. We cannot subject ourselves to the scandal of divorce."

"Of course not," she said, muted.

"Now, that did not stop my parents from having affairs."

The very thought sent a burst of strange pain through her body. "I have no interest in affairs," she said stiffly.

"Such is your devotion for me?"

"I see no need for it," she said. "It opens us up to pointless censure. The sort of thing we don't need."

"Well then," he said. "Feel free to conduct your business as you see fit."

"And yours?"

"Sadly for you, you are not in a power position."

He was correct. It was the thing that galled her so badly. She had used him. She had used the opportunity presented before her, because how could she not. But Gunnar had only been on his back foot for a few moments, and now it was clear that his was the position of power.

He had been intending to marry anyway, and whether or not it was her or anyone else would hardly matter to him. In fact, all she had done was deliver him an easier bride.

She was the one who would be grafted into a life she had not wanted.

Finding herself potentially shackled to a man she didn't even like.

But you are fascinated by him…

It didn't matter. He was ridiculous. A disreputable playboy.

With a multibillion-dollar company?

That made her wonder if there was more to him.

But she still couldn't… She couldn't fathom sharing a life with him. She could barely share a room with him without wanting to throw something heavy at him.

"I suppose…" She took a breath. This was the only part that would salvage it for her. The one thing that she wanted, above all else. "I suppose there will be children."

"No," he said, firm and decisive.

That shocked her. So much so she couldn't believe he'd said them. "What?"

"I've no desire for children."

The word settled over her skin, a strange, buzzing sensation filling her ears. "You're a prince. Surely you must produce heirs."

"My sister has done so already."

"What if something were to happen to him? God forbid, Gunnar, but it must be considered."

"She will have more children. She and that husband of hers will likely fill the palace. He is Italian."

"That is an incorrigible thing to say."

"I am incorrigible." He shrugged a shoulder. "My father was a tyrant. My time spent in a father-son relationship was unendurable. I have no interest in revisiting it. I have no interest at all in being father to anyone or anything. That word is forever tainted for me. And, as I have no need of producing children…"

"But think of what it would do for your standing in the media."

"Oh, I daresay they will be fine taking photographs of us at various parties. You will be the envy of women the world over."

"Because I'm with you?"

"Obviously." He lifted a shoulder. "I'm rich and handsome. Titled as well. You will be a style icon because you are my wife. Many women would have wanted such an honor. And you have it now."

"But no children."

"Surely your position as one of the top influencers in the world will compensate for that."

Anger vibrated in her core, but she said nothing.

This was worse than she could've possibly imagined. She had not simply trapped herself in a marriage, but she had trapped herself in a childless one. She wanted to be a mother. To fulfill that loneliness inside of her. To repair the distance that she had always felt in her relationship with her own parents, by being a better mother to her children.

And he was not allowing it. He was taking this from her.

It was a thing she could not endure.

But what could she do? She was completely and utterly trapped. Between a madman, and one who had just laid down an edict for her life that she did not know if she can survive. Still, she would have to take Gunnar. Because the alternative may very well actually kill her.

"Well," she said. "If there are to be no children, and you are happy to have affairs. Then I see no point in the two of us having sexual relationships."

Something in his gaze changed. It turned to ice. And then to blue flame. "Is that what you think?"

"As you said. You do not see any reason for a couple in our position to stay faithful, as your parents did not."

"And you think that you can resist me?" he asked.

He was utterly sincere. And she would love to laugh in his face.

Sadly, she wasn't immune to his body, whatever she might want to believe. In fact, his body transfixed her in ways no other man's ever had. Even now, even as he dashed her dreams of the future to dust, she couldn't deny the attraction that flared inside of her.

"It may have escaped your notice, but I have done an admirable job of resisting you for the past three years." That at least was true. She hadn't—as far as she knew—

ever really betrayed her attraction to him. He might suspect, but he didn't know.

"Well, that is because I have never truly tried to seduce you."

She sniffed. "You do have a very high opinion of yourself."

"Well, ask yourself this, Latika. When you needed a port in the storm, where did you look? You looked to me. And I would suggest that that makes me perhaps a bit more than you would like me to be."

"I think perhaps your mind makes you a bit more than you are."

"However you like. Don't think I don't recognize the heat between us. And don't think I don't realize that it is mutual. Whatever I feel for you...you feel it for me."

"How do you know I feel a thing for you?" she asked.

"You were awfully comfortable coming up and kissing me."

Heat stung her face. Shame lashing her like a whip. "When people are in burning buildings, they are awfully comfortable jumping out of five-story windows hoping that they land favorably. I was willing to take my chances with you."

"Call me whatever you like," he said. "A panic button. The fire you jumped to from the frying pan. A last resort. But your mouth doesn't lie when it touches mine. It may when you speak, but you cannot deny chemistry such as ours. Not where it counts."

"I can."

Because he was denying her children. And so, she would deny him her body. There was perhaps no convincing him she didn't want him, but that didn't mean she would weaken in her resolve.

He stared at her, hard. Those blue eyes seeming to look beneath her clothes, beneath her skin. Her heart was thundering, her whole body beginning to tremble. Why did he affect her like this? How?

"You truly expect that we will be married for the rest of our lives and never explore this chemistry between us?" he asked.

She had no defenses left. None but the truth. "It should be no hardship to me. After all, I've reached the age of twenty-four without ever having been with a man. What's twenty-four more years?"

"I did not realize you were so young," he said, his expression strange.

"I don't advertise. Do you think my parents waited until I was very old to try and marry me off? Of course they didn't. They had dynasties to try and make."

"You think we'll only be married twenty-four years? That's not very much time for the rest of your life."

"I was thinking yours," she said, her tone stiff. "After all, your age is much more advanced than mine. And also, I may poison you."

He shrugged. The casual, disaffected gesture such a stereotype she wanted to hit him. "So long as it's in a good whiskey, I may not even mind."

"No commentary on the state of my hymen?"

"I'm not surprised," he said dismissively. "Given how frosty you are, it's little wonder."

Damn. The. Man.

"Well then. It seems that you're not missing anything by being denied my bed and my body. In fact, you should be very happy."

"Consider me overjoyed. I may find a porn star to celebrate our engagement with."

"It's neither here nor there to me, Gunnar. Provided you practice discretion. But then, that's your part. The improving of your reputation. All I need is to be saved."

"I hope you enjoy planning your wedding. We haven't been able to hire you a replacement."

The man was made of ice. She had expected him to protest...to...to something... Act surprised when she threw her virginity down as a gauntlet.

To act disappointed when she said she wouldn't sleep with him, which wounded her feminine pride in ways she would rather not admit. But no. He reacted to nothing.

And he never wanted children.

"Do you care for anyone?" she asked. "Do you even care for your sister really?"

"What does the evidence tell you, darling? For while you may not be able to lie with your body, I can lie with anything I want. I will be much more likely to trust you than me in any situation."

"Well, then I will continue to do so."

She would have to trust herself. She might have used Gunnar, but she couldn't trust him. She would have to remember that. She could trust only herself. And in that regard, while many things felt different in her life at this moment, that one truth remained. She had to rely on herself. And she would. Because she was strong. That truth was the only thing that kept her from slipping completely into despair.

CHAPTER SIX

LATIKA WAS A VIRGIN. Or so she claimed. She was also intent on denying him access to her body. Clearly the last-ditch effort of feelings of control in the situation. Or maybe, an attempt to punish him.

Or maybe… Maybe she truly did not desire him in the way that he did her.

But, that seemed unlikely.

Twenty-four.

She seemed much older than that.

All these revelations had shocked him to his core. And yet, he could not allow her to see it. And she had the nerve to ask him if he even cared for his sister. She had no idea. No idea of why he lived the way he did. He had done everything he could to protect Astrid, not just from his father. But everything he was supposed to learn in his father's name. What Gunnar's father had tried to teach was an abomination.

His father had tried to plant the idea in his mind that women were inferior to men. He'd tried to poison Gunnar's mind. The cost of his resistance had been great.

Latika thought she knew who he was, based on the lies he'd told the world about himself. She was clearly under the impression that he was every inch the debauched playboy.

It could not stand.

He was going to take her to his office in the States. He would show her what he was.

He couldn't tell her. Not everything. Not about his father. But he could show her that he was more.

But he would wait. He would wait until after their wedding. Because the thing that he wanted more than anything in the world was the chance to prove her wrong using nothing more than her own body.

She thought she was kept at night stewing in her irritation over him, but he knew differently.

She was only a woman. And he was only a man. Neither of them were above the basic biology that demanded their bodies mate.

Of course, thinking of it in terms of biology brought him back to the moment Latika had thrown down her virginity revelation.

It had been when he said they would not have children.

He wondered if that was related strictly to practicality, or if for some sort of emotional attachment to the idea of having children herself.

He supposed it wasn't that surprising, given the fact that many women seemed to want children. Most women, he would have thought, would consider a prince enough of a consolation prize. Though, Latika seemed bound and determined to punish him.

She had been avoiding him since the night of the ball. Throwing herself into the melee of planning the wedding.

Meanwhile, Gunnar had been concentrating on the media component.

"There's the groom to be."

He looked up and saw Astrid standing there. She was dressed immaculately, her red hair pulled back into a tight bun.

"Yes. Here I am."

He had been avoiding her since the announcement. Mostly because he didn't want to get into a discussion. He didn't want her questioning him.

She did so, out of habit. A feeling that she was the oldest, and therefore the protector.

"You've been avoiding me," she pointed out.

"Yes," he agreed. "I have definitely been avoiding you."

"Why?"

"Related to the impending lecture."

"How did you know?" She asked, narrowing her eyes at him.

"Oh, just a feeling I had. I was right, wasn't I?"

"I want to be sure that you don't hurt her."

"Interesting," he said. "A different lecture to the one I expected to receive."

"Oh, you expected me to say that you should be on guard in case Latika hurts you? We both know that is impossible."

And he was left to wonder how the whole world seemed to think of him as heartless. Even by a sister he'd worked so hard to save.

"I've no designs on hurting her. She seems a nice woman."

"You're attracted to her. She's attracted to you. But you need to understand that she's inexperienced and…"

"How do you know?"

"Well, I don't really. But, the things that she said seem to imply as much."

He thought of what Latika had said to him. That she had not been with a man in her whole twenty-four years of life.

That, combined with what Astrid said, made him wonder if it was true. "It may surprise you to learn that Latika has already laid out her ground rules. Which, include staying out of my bed."

Astrid frowned. "Really?"

"We are not a love match, Astrid, as you well know. We can barely tolerate being in the same room as each other."

"But she… Yes. But as you so eloquently put it earlier, you… You're attracted to each other."

"It's obvious, I'd think. But, she would happily slit my throat in bed after. Believe me."

"She turned to you when she needed help."

"A person will take their chances with the pavement below when they're trapped in a high-rise building during a fire." He repeated Latika's words back to his sister.

"Oh."

"I'm sorry, you don't need to interfere. The both of us can handle ourselves."

Astrid sighed. "Yes. My concern is that you won't be able to handle each other."

"Dear sister, I make it my business to handle women."

"But Latika is not like your other women. And you will be stuck with her. So whatever you do, you will have to face the aftermath of it. You're not good with consequences, Gunnar."

Just like that, he heard his father's voice echoing in his head. And he was flooded by memories. Days spent in the dungeon of the palace.

Day after day. Spent in isolation, in starvation.

There will be consequences, Gunnar. If you cannot take on board my lessons.

And there had been. Painful consequences.

"No," he said, grinning. "I'm absolutely terrible with consequences. In that I tend not to acknowledge them"

"What about children?"

A poignant question, considering what was on his mind. "There won't be children."

"Why not?"

"Astrid, you know what our childhood was like. I have no desire to father children."

"I love being a mother," she said.

"We lived different childhoods," he said.

"Yes," Astrid said. "I know. Father distrusted me. Mother supported me. She ignored you. But father..."

"You think that I enjoyed getting attention from a man who despised my sister?"

Astrid blinked. "I didn't... I didn't think that might be a problem."

"Of course it is," he said. "You are like a part of me. You are my twin. We are blood in a way few other people on this earth are. Whatever father wanted from me, he was not going to get it."

"That doesn't mean that you shouldn't have children."

"Oh, there are many reasons I shouldn't have children. That's only one of them."

"That breaks my heart," she said.

"It doesn't break mine. I am perfectly happy watching you with your life. Latika and I have come to an agreement. We will live separate lives. I will protect her, she will enrich my reputation. There is nothing to dislike about it."

"If you say so."

"I do. You might rule the country, Astrid, but in my own life, my word is law."

"Of course. I have never thought differently." What he didn't tell his sister was that he wasn't content with the idea of keeping their lives separate. Not completely.

Because he was not a man given to taking commands. Was not a man who bowed to the will of others.

No.

His father had tried. He had tried and tried to break him. But it had forged Gunnar into the strongest steel imaginable.

As his new bride would soon discover.

Yes. Latika would discover it soon enough.

Latika was carried away on the tide of the farce she was currently engaged in. Completely overwhelmed by her role as bride, and retreating as often as possible into the role of planner. It was easy to make decisions when she divorced herself from the narrative. When she thought of it as planning a royal wedding in the generic sense. Rather than her own.

Not that it mattered what her own personal preference was. Not in the context of this arrangement. What mattered was the spectacle. What mattered, was that she took herself out of harm's way. Whether or not she enjoyed the look of the wedding didn't come into it at all.

But there was one piece of it that she found impossible to divorce her emotions, and indeed her body from. And that was the acquisition of a wedding gown.

She asked Astrid to be there when she made her selection. In part because Astrid was acting as her maid of honor. A farce it might be, but it was a real wedding. And Astrid was her real friend. Much more than Gunnar could ever be considered a real fiancé.

Well, he was real in the sense that she was going to marry him.

She supposed that was the only sense that mattered.

"That one's pretty," Astrid said, but her tone said she did not think it was all that pretty.

Latika looked at herself critically in the mirror. The dress was not to her taste at all, and didn't look particularly flattering on her. For that reason alone, part of her wanted to choose it.

But there would also be pictures, and she was vain enough to not want photographs of her looking anything less than beautiful circulating the world.

But then, maybe she could still find something that didn't feel too personal.

"What I think doesn't matter," Astrid said. "It should be about you."

"It shouldn't be," Latika said. "It is about the spectacle of the royal wedding. It's about putting out into the world what we must."

"And you don't have feelings for my brother." Astrid said, her tone incisive. "Not at all?"

Latika's neck prickled. "It's complicated."

"Is it? It all seems very straightforward to me. Ragnar was at the palace. And I'm very sorry that we failed you in that way."

"Don't apologize to me," Latika said. "The fact of the matter is, I was never going to escape him forever. And I knew it."

"But I said that we would protect you…"

"And you did. You have. And now the crown is protecting me further."

"He told me that you… That you want the marriage to be in name only."

Latika's face flamed. "Why would he tell you that?"

"You may have noticed that my brother doesn't keep secrets."

"Well, it would've been nice of him to keep that to himself," Latika grumbled.

"Why won't you make it a real marriage?"

Latika swallowed. "He doesn't want children. He also said that there was no reason for us to be faithful to one another. If he intends that we sleep with other people, and the two of us don't even have to produce a child, then why bother with each other at all?"

"He *said that* to you?" Astrid asked, incredulous.

"Yes."

"He's an idiot. And I think that he has feelings for you."

Latika laughed. "The only feelings we have for each other are antagonistic. Whatever narrative you've made up in your mind about the two of us… It isn't real. And I appreciate so much that you care about me. About him. You are better than either of us deserve, Astrid. You have been so wonderful to us. But he and I have never had interaction beyond what you've seen. There is nothing secret happening."

"I believe you," Astrid said.

"Your tone says you think I'm telling the truth, but that you don't think I know my own mind."

"I just don't want you to get hurt."

"Believe me. My options are such that I don't fear

any pain from Gunnar." Latika paused for a moment. "You were asking me for advice."

"Well," Astrid said. "I'm married now."

"And I'm still a woman running from overbearing parents and an abusive former fiancé. No offense meant, Astrid, but your relationship with Mauro does not make you an expert on the feelings of every person."

"None taken at all," Astrid said.

But Latika could tell that Astrid still didn't believe her, and she thought it best to say nothing at all. Instead, they continued to rifle through the racks of gowns that had been given to them.

"You should try this," Astrid said, holding up a devastatingly beautiful gown, deceptively simple, and made from the finest white satin. It had long, flowing sleeves and a square neck, a fitted bodice and a skirt that flared out at the bottom.

It was perfect. Sophisticated and sleek, and absolutely something she would've chosen for a wedding to a man she had chosen.

"This one," Astrid said, decisively.

Latika decided she would try it on. But she wasn't certain if she could bring herself to choose it.

The day of the wedding was ominous. Clouds hung thick and low over the mountains, a dramatic effect, the dark green trees piercing through the mist, making it look as if the hills had teeth.

Truly, not an auspicious day for a wedding. But Gunnar did not believe in such things.

He had never been given cause to believe in love at all.

And this was no different. It was not luck that had

brought him here. It was simply a twist of fate, one that he was fine enough to lean into.

He had allowed Latika to continue to evade him up until today. But tonight, tonight he would launch an all-out seduction of her senses.

Why? To prove that you can manipulate her? How does that make you any different than him?

He ignored that inner voice.

He didn't want to manipulate her. He wanted to seduce her. He wanted her. And they were going to be married. The idea that they would only sleep with other people seemed foolish to him, and he had been prepared to offer his wife his fidelity.

He had only said those things to her to get to her, and in many ways, he imagined she had done the same with him. He sincerely doubted that she was actually going to hold to her missish cries anyway. Just as he sincerely doubted she was actually a virgin. The more he thought about it, the more he thought that conversation was designed to give her a power position.

Of course, she would remember that he had said he didn't want a virgin bride. And for whatever reason, she was attempting to prove to him that she was unsuitable in some way.

And again, he felt that had to be about power, rather than any kind of sincere desire to put him off. She needed him to marry her. And given that truth, he didn't actually take any of her nonsense terribly seriously.

He turned and looked in the mirror.

A black suit.

The very thing she told him he didn't require help with for the ball.

He imagined that at that point she had no idea that

the next place she would be seeing him in a suit was their wedding.

He certainly hadn't.

With the decisiveness of a predator, Gunnar turned and walked out of the room, prowling down the halls, making his way to the chapel that was on the grounds of the palace.

Theirs was not a wedding with quite as much fanfare as his sister's. After all, the wedding of the Queen, particularly to someone as famous and outrageous as Mauro, had been an insane spectacle. But, there had been a bit of something as well. The paparazzi was fascinated by her, and of course, a profile had been released about her in the media. Information about her family. They had interviewed her parents, who'd had nothing but good things to say about their daughter.

And he knew that they had contacted the palace and asked for an invitation.

It was a decision that Gunnar had been hard-pressed to make. Because, on the one hand, her parents had clearly tormented her by putting her in the path of Ragnar. But on the other, this marriage solved all of their issues. And keeping her parents away from the wedding might only cause tension, and give Ragnar a foothold.

Indeed, it might also make her parents into problems that he didn't want to deal with. So with regret, he had given them an invite.

He could only hope he didn't regret it. The church was filled already, hundreds of guests in attendance, and millions tuning in on television, and on the computer. And Astrid met him outside the sanctuary.

"Why aren't you already seated?"

"We walk together," she said. She looked up at him,

her green eyes filled with emotion. "I noticed you did not have a best man. Well, I am your twin. And there is no one on this earth who has ever been closer to you than me. So I will walk with you."

His sister's sentimentality hit him hard. At the same time, made great tendrils of acidic emotion churn through his stomach. Because she thought they were close. She thought they shared a bond he wasn't entirely certain they did. She thought she knew him. When he had kept so much back from her. For her own protection.

And yet, she was standing with him. And that mattered. He would let the other things fall from his mind. They walked to the front of the sanctuary together, whispers filling the air, heads turning as they moved. And then he took his position at the head of the altar.

Astrid nodded her head regally, and then went and took her seat by her husband.

Gunnar was very accomplished at not paying attention in church, and he handily tuned out the exhortation given by the priest, and the hymn that went up after. And then, it was time for the bride to walk down the aisle.

The music shifted, swelled, and after a few moments, Latika appeared. Her long black hair was swept up in a bun, her gown made of lace and glimmering beads, the skirt heavy and full, rising and falling elegantly with each step she took. She was an uncommon beauty. And as she walked toward him, his plan became blurry.

Because it was difficult to think straight with Latika there.

Difficult to have a clear-eyed view of his plan. In fact he forgot his plan. Forgot there was anything other than this stark, physical need igniting a fire inside of him. He was in a church, but his thoughts were decidedly less than pure.

In fact, he would not have been surprised to burst into flame at any moment. And when she joined him at the head of the altar, looking all stiff and uncomfortable, he wanted to kiss away those grim lines around her mouth. Wanted to crush her up against his body and kiss her until neither of them could breathe. He already knew how intoxicating a kiss between them could be. How could she deny them? Both of them? They wanted each other, and she was intent on...playing games. Well, it would not stand. She was using him, and he could fully respect that. But that didn't mean she got to be the only one with a say in how their marriage would be conducted.

She turned to face him, wordless. And they both stayed silent until the part came for them to repeat their vows.

It was easy for him, because he had never taken much of anything to heart, or treated anything with reverence, so he didn't know why this should be any different.

Latika, for her part, seemed stilted.

Then she looked over, and he could see the exact moment her eyes came to rest on her parents.

Her face went scarlet, her eyes widening with shock.

She finished out her vows tightlipped.

And when time came for the kiss, he determined that he would do his part in loosening that terse expression.

She might not want to desire him, but the fact of the matter was, she did. And he was going to use that.

He lowered his head, capturing her in his arms and holding her firmly against his body. Then he lowered his head and kissed her.

It was nothing like the other two kisses they had shared. For now, they had an audience, it was true. But he was fully in command of the situation.

And it was Latika who melted beneath the heat between them. He crushed her lips beneath his, and forced them apart, sliding his tongue against hers. She was sweet. She was so very sweet.

A prickly, intoxicating beauty.

One that had resisted him far longer than anyone else ever had. One that made his heart beat faster. Made it feel like his body was on fire, and how long had it been since a woman had interested him in such a way?

He couldn't remember.

His image was a blur of glitter, golden brown and red lips. Latika was the only woman in his memory. The only woman that he wanted. He knew that his kiss was pushing the bonds of propriety for a royal wedding—many royal couples did not engage in physical affection such as this, even during the wedding ceremony.

But he didn't care.

As far as he was concerned, being a married man was more legitimate than he had ever intended to be, and he wouldn't be denied this pleasure. Not now. Not now that he finally had her—Latika—beneath his lips.

And it was only a taste. Only a taste of what was to come later. He wanted her. My God how he wanted this woman. It defied everything. Every basic idea he'd ever had about himself.

The world that he lived in where women were interchangeable and one soft body was as good as the next.

Except, no one would do but her. Not now.

When they parted, he was breathing hard. Latika, for her part, was a blank space.

The priest pronounced them man and wife, and he and Latika held onto each other's arms, and walked down the aisle. Once they were free of the audience, free of the church, she jerked away from him.

"How dare you not tell me my parents would be here?"

"I'm sorry," he said. "I miscalculated your response to that. I did not think it would matter."

"How could you think it wouldn't matter? I haven't seen them in more than three years."

"I thought it wouldn't matter because I thought you were a woman of some intellect. One who understood that sometimes the benefits to something outweigh the potential costs. If your parents feel that this marriage will give them more than what your marriage to Ragnar would give, then they will engage in the protection of it as well. You no longer have anything to fear from them. However, should we have excluded them from the happy event, I fear that they might have retaliated. It is all about ensuring that this gives them more than he could have. You must understand that."

She looked away from him, her throat working. "I understand. But you should have told me."

"Perhaps you should have warned me that we were going to get engaged two weeks ago."

"I didn't know..."

"And I simply made a decision when it came across my desk, Latika. One that I thought was best."

"I can't stand this. *I can't stand this*." She exploded, all her reserve gone now. And not in the way he'd wanted. "None of my life is in my control. And I fear that it never will be."

"Are any of our lives ever in our control?"

"You're a prince," she sputtered, straightening her hands down at her sides, smacking against her full skirt. "You're a man. You have full control over your life. Control to disobey. Control to do whatever you like."

He grabbed hold of her arm and drew her close, something inside of him snapping. "You have no idea what my life has been like. You have no idea what I have been allowed to do, and not allowed to do. Or why I have made the decisions I've made. Do not speak to me about all the freedom you think I have."

He released his hold on her then, as the doors to the sanctuary opened, and Astrid appeared. Along with Mauro. And their child.

"Is everything all right?"

"Gunnar surprised me with a visit from my parents," Latika said, her tone wooden.

"I thought you knew," Astrid said.

"No."

Astrid treated him to an icy glare.

"I refuse to stand in between the two of you when you do that," Gunnar said. "I'm not a naughty child to be scolded. I made a decision that I thought would best protect my wife, Astrid. I will thank you to not undermine me."

His sister looked shocked, but said nothing.

"We are also not attending the reception," he continued.

Astrid looked doubly shocked at that. "What?"

"We are going away on our honeymoon. My wife clearly doesn't wish to be bothered by her parents. They have been given what they wanted. Access to the palace. I assume, Astrid, that you can make them feel welcome, while Latika gets a reprieve."

"Yes," Astrid said. "I can definitely do that."

"Good. Astrid will see to everything," he said to Latika. "Unless you wish to speak to your parents."

"No. I've made a life for myself, a space for myself where I'm not a pawn. And because of them...well, because of them, here we are. I have nothing to say to them."

"Well, this should handle them once and for all, shouldn't it? In the meantime, I have already taken the liberty of packing your things."

"Why are you doing this?" she asked. "You left the entire planning of the wedding to me, and now you're pulling rank?"

"Because, my dear. You're about to discover exactly how this protection is going to work. If you seek shelter with me, then you must deal with my commands. I'm terribly sorry if that interferes in some way with your preferences. But I am not a boy to be manipulated. You leapt out of the burning building into my arms, Latika. And now you must contend with the consequences."

And that was how Latika found herself thirty thousand feet in the air in Gunnar's lavish private jet. She had been in it before, once, when she had needed to meet Astrid somewhere in Europe, when they had been separated. She had thought it gaudy and extravagant then. She did not think it any better now.

Astrid's was all clean lines and taupe leather. Gunnar's was gold and black, a large bed at the center.

"Well, I see you haven't updated," she said waspishly, sitting down on one of the plush leather chairs, designed for a person to sink into the material. Rather than for lovely, modern form.

"It's comfortable," he said. "I believe in substance over style. When it comes to my furniture. In terms of myself, I obviously go with style. But something has to have substance."

"When did you plan for us to leave directly after the wedding?"

"The moment we were standing there and I saw how upset you were."

She couldn't tell if he was sincere. With Gunnar it was nearly impossible to tell. And yet it did something to her stomach to hear him say that. "Really."

"Yes," he said. "I did not mean to distress you by inviting your parents to the wedding. What I told you is true. I genuinely believed that it was the best thing. But there is no reason you should have to socialize with them. Anyway, I was already planning on taking you to the States for a honeymoon. And so that you could see my company."

"New York?"

"No," he said. "San Diego."

That surprised her. But, she also felt just slightly relieved that she didn't have to return to New York. She hadn't been since she had fled her family. And the idea of leaving her parents behind in his land, only to return to a place that she associated with her stifling upbringing didn't suit her.

"I've never been to California," she said.

"How is that possible?"

"We didn't travel that direction. We went to Europe often. Up and down the eastern seaboard. To India. We never had occasion to go to California."

"You'll like it," he said.

"How can you possibly say that with such certainty?" Like he knew her.

"Because it's different than Bjornland. It will be a nice change of pace. For one thing, the ocean is there."

She did miss the ocean. She had always adored visiting the atmospheric beaches of the Atlantic back home. And she adored Goa on holiday. Being introduced to another beach would be nice.

But she was still feeling angry at him, and determined not to allow him to see that she thought it might be nice at all.

It was sour of her, perhaps. But she still felt so very...

Fragile. And a bit like upon being moved around on a chessboard.

Is that fair? You are the one who went to him for help. For this kind of help. You backed him into a corner, and now you're angry with him.

Well. Yes. She was. She couldn't deny that.

"I still don't understand how you managed to keep that a secret."

"And like I told you, people don't go looking for something reputable when someone is wandering around throwing the disreputable in their face. They assume, of course that what I'd like to hide is my scandalous behavior. No one can quite comprehend the fact that I don't care much about that at all. Who would think to look for success?"

"But you go into the office and..."

"Sometimes. Everyone who works there has signed a gag order."

"You're kidding."

"I'm not. Of course, we will be doing away with all of that now. We will be making our debut at the company as husband and wife, and we will be having a proper show for the media. Where all will be revealed."

"Including why you hid it?"

He shook his head. "No. That's not a story I'll ever tell."

"Will you tell me?" Her question seemed to land in a dead space of air. Changing the feel of the room.

Ice blue eyes rested on hers. "No."

She suddenly felt frustrated. She couldn't get a read on him. It was as if this thing she had thought was a puddle all along had turned out to be a fathomless sea. She couldn't see the bottom. And she could not figure out how she had thought it was a puddle in the first place either.

And all of it left her feeling confused, and for a woman who was already feeling at the end of her tether with not knowing what to do in a situation, it was all a bit much.

"I made the right decision, then," she said.

"And that is what?"

"The decision to not share my body with you."

His gaze sharpened. "You think?"

"Yes. Because if you can't even share with me the story of why you started this company, then I don't know how we could ever share anything else."

"Are you so naïve that you imagine a meeting of bodies must also be a meeting of souls?"

She tilted her chin upward, her heart pounding heavily. "I already told you. I'm a virgin. So I wouldn't really know."

"I don't believe you," he said.

Of all the possible responses to that, this was not what she had imagined. "You don't believe me?"

"No. I think you're telling me that because I told you I didn't want to marry a virgin."

"Not everything is about you," she said. "My virginity certainly isn't."

"I don't believe that. Surely most things are about me."

"No, I hate to disappoint you."

"You don't kiss like a virgin."

Her stomach twisted. "How do I kiss?"

"Well, mostly like an indignant cat who would like to scratch my eyes out, and scratch my back, but isn't sure which she wants more."

"Well, that's close enough to the mark," she said.

"So you do want to leave claw marks down my back. Little virgin, that seems like something you couldn't possibly handle."

"If you're trying to goad me into sex, then you've badly miscalculated."

"I'm not trying to goad you into anything. Goading you is simply the natural way we communicate. I assumed it was our love language."

"I'm tired," she said.

She was. But that wasn't the primary reason she needed to be done with this. Because she felt too wounded, too raw, too fragile to deal with him.

"There's a bed just there."

"I won't share it with you."

"Fine by me. I've no interest in sleeping next to you."

"Why do you want me?" Her frustration boiled over. It made no sense. He made no sense. Why did he want her in particular? Particularly after all this time? Why did it seem to be her specifically? They didn't like each other. They didn't get along. And yet something drew her to him, and she could blame her lack of experience. But he... He could have his pick of women who didn't fight with him. Who didn't irritate him. So why he should want her... She just didn't know.

Suddenly, it was as if a wall dropped between them. "I don't know," he said, his voice rough. "And if I had an answer, perhaps I would not feel so driven to get you underneath me. But I don't know. I don't understand it. I have wanted you with a ferocity that defied logic ever since the first time I saw you. And then you opened your mouth, and I wanted, in equal parts to argue with you. I've never understood either compulsion."

Those eyes were such an intense blue. "People don't compel me, Latika. They don't make me do anything. You... You bring out responses in myself that even I don't understand. I don't like it."

She swallowed hard, her heart hammering. "I don't understand how a person can want to slap someone and kiss them."

"I think you and I have far too much chemistry," he said. "The good and the bad. And there doesn't seem to be very clear reason as to why it's so strong."

The talk of chemistry with that big bed right over there, with no escape, terrified her. Because there really was nothing holding her back from being with him.

Yes, there was her sense of self-preservation. Her desire to control the situation in which she had none. But... But she wanted him. And the question now was if she was truly intent on cutting off his nose and hers, which would spite his face, but hers as well.

The look in those blue eyes nearly undid her. And she nearly went to him. Nearly shamed herself by crawling onto his lap, pressing her mouth to his so that she might get another chance to taste him.

But then it hit her. That he was just another jailer. And the last thing she wanted was to end up with feelings for him. She had loved her parents, but it had not changed the fact that she'd been used by them.

This line of thinking made her head throb, because yes, she had been using Gunnar as well. But she was very afraid that her feelings were vulnerable to changing. That she might find herself caring for him, while he simply saw her as a means to an end. A man who had said his vows in a church, without blinking, while he had already made it very plain to her that he had no intention of keeping them.

"I'm tired," she reiterated. "I'm going to sleep."

CHAPTER SEVEN

WHEN LATIKA WOKE, the plane had touched down in San Diego and when she exited the plane, she was stunned by the brilliant blue. The sea, the sky. The Pacific in all its glory.

The sun on her skin was perfection.

She loved her adopted country, but it was a very cold climate. And even though she was used to the intensity of East Coast winters, she had always preferred blue skies.

She could definitely see why Gunnar had chosen to position his business here.

But, she didn't want to tell him that.

"We can go to my house. And then, we will continue on to take the tour of the business."

"You have a house here?" she asked.

"Of course I do. It would be a very silly thing to have offices here, and no house, don't you think?"

She realized that she had imagined that everything Gunnar did was silly. So, it had truly never occurred to her that there could be such hidden depths to him.

"You don't have to tell me the story," she said as they got into the limo that had met them. "But will you at least tell me why you have gone to such great lengths to play the part of court jester, when you're a prince."

"Court jester? I always thought I was quite like Prince Harry."

"Prince Harry is less shameless."

"You must understand," he said, his voice grave. "My father did not want my sister to rule the country. We were twins, with her born five minutes before me. And he did not feel that was sufficient reason to be denied the male heir that he felt the country deserved. My sister had to work so hard to prove to him that she was capable. And I did everything in my power to make them think that I might not be capable."

"All of this… It was a ruse for your father?"

"Not all. But yes, that certainly played into it."

"And you started the business because…"

"Because I was bored. Because a man of my age cannot be happy bouncing from club to club, and bed to bed of anonymous women endlessly."

"Can't they? It seems to me that a great many men would like you to think that they can."

"Without exception, I find the people with the widest smiles on their faces in establishments like that have the biggest holes inside of them."

"Including you?"

He lifted a shoulder. "I'm not entirely convinced that if you knocked on my chest it wouldn't sound hollow."

And yet, it was increasingly difficult for Latika to believe that. She thought that he wanted the world to believe it, but that he wasn't strictly true. She had called into question his caring about his sister, and she regretted that. She regretted it quite bitterly, because she had watched him play the role of protector to Astrid, in spite of the fact that his sister technically inhabited a loftier position than he did. She had the distinct feeling that Gunnar would risk his life for her.

"I don't think it's hollow," she said.

"Don't you?"

"You're helping me."

"I'm helping myself," he responded.

"Yes," she said. "I suppose so."

But there was something in the way he said all that that made her question things. And one of the biggest was if his heart was truly a hollow place, or if the real issue was that it was too full of something darker, that he refused to talk about.

The location of Gunnar's company surprised her. It wasn't situated in the Gaslamp Quarter, or in the business district of downtown. Rather, it was somewhere near old town, back up in the hills and overlooking the ocean. The entire place was built into the side of the mountain, made from shipping containers, glass cut into it, running from floor to ceiling. Parts of it were fashioned with wings from an old Boeing 747, creating a light, steel roof with strange and interesting curves. It blended in with the mountain, just the slightest link of shine, that seemed reflected again in the crystal-clear waves of the Pacific.

"This isn't what I expected," she said.

"Why would anything I do be expected?" he asked.

"I haven't the faintest idea."

The car wound up beside of the mountain, the wide, paved road offering a smooth, easy ride.

What surprised her, more than the appearance of the containers themselves, was that inside it was the epitome of modernity. Neutrals, and incredible natural light filtering in through all the glass and reflecting off the chrome beams that ran the length of the ceiling. The curves, and light metal of the wing that served as the roof offering strange interest to the place, which was more artiste than office.

He smiled when they entered. "Good morning," he said.

There were a great many staff, right there in the room. The building was open, with desks situated all around.

"Good morning," of course came back.

"Is there any news to report?" he asked.

"None," one of the women sitting nearest the door said. She was looking sideways at Gunnar, a questioning expression on her face.

"This is my wife," he said.

"We know that," one of the men toward the back said. "Your wedding was international news. Not that any of us could talk about the fact that we know you."

"I've been avoiding all mentions of it," one of the women said. "I didn't want to let anything slip."

"Well," Gunnar said. "Now you don't have to worry about it. Because the press is going to be here in the next ten minutes. We're going to go on a tour of the facility. This place isn't a secret anymore. The good news is for your trouble, you will all be getting raises."

A cheer erupted from the desks. And Latika couldn't get over just how comfortable everyone seemed to be with him. There was an ease to his interactions with all of these people that she would never have expected to find.

They all spoke to him not even just like he was a normal boss, but like he was a normal person.

Gunnar was neither of those things. Latika couldn't even squint and turn upside down to look at him and pretend it was so.

Latika did a brief circuit of the room, being introduced to everyone here in this portion of the office, and that was when the first reporter arrived.

All told, there were four of them, with cameras and recorders. And they followed Latika and Gunnar around the office, while he made broad, sweeping gestures and talked about the work this company had been doing for years, the strides they had made in both green energy and building.

Innovations that Latika knew about, but that she'd had no idea had been financed by research Gunnar had done.

"Why the secrecy?" One of the reporters asked when they reached the very top shipping crate, that was up two flights of stairs, nestled into a higher part of the mountain. The whole thing served as Gunnar's office, his desk overlooking the pristine ocean.

He was a man that always seemed at ease in his own skin. But here there was something more to it. This was his. The palace in Bjornland was decorated in tradition. And there were updates done now, but they were Astrid's.

This was Gunnar.

Large and at ease. Civilized. But with only a thin veneer between that civility and the wild, raging ocean.

"For a long while I felt it would distract from my efforts. My reputation has never been sterling. And I needed investors. Backers. People who would throw me their best researchers, so that we could make these things happen."

She had a feeling that the words slipping off his tongue were a lie. Very nice lies that everyone around them seemed to be swallowing.

But she didn't.

"And why is this a particular area of interest for you?" one of the reporters asked.

"Bjornland is one of the best examples of the majesty of nature. I grew up surrounded by mountains. Clear sky. I have always loved the outdoors. And I have always felt passionate about preserving it. You may know that I was part of creating a preserve in my home country that left many of the mountains off-limits to development."

He continued. "I was part of that effort in my late teens, and it is something that I found a great deal of satisfaction in. Going out and drinking the night away is fun, but there is little left of that good time in the morning. To be able to invest in something that will last, and to make that investment in the world that we all live in, that is the best thing I can think to do with my money. And it has been a profitable endeavor. Do not imagine that I am entirely altruistic. I assure you that I'm not." He laughed. "But, being with Latika has inspired me to live differently."

"And so the timing of this reveal does coincide with the wedding?" one of the reporters asked.

"How could it not?" Gunnar asked. "It has changed me. This marriage. Being with her. I can make of no better way to mark that, than by laying bare every aspect of who I am. I had to do it with her before we wed. The good and the ugly. I feel that the whole world is fairly apprised of my ugly. For Latika's sake, if nothing else, perhaps more of my good should be out there as well."

He took a few more questions, and then he dismissed them, leaving Gunnar and herself alone in the office.

"Is that all true?" she asked, her voice small in the large space. "About your investment in these projects?"

"Yes," he said. "I blackmailed my father for that preserve. I hope you know."

"You what?"

"I was eighteen, and he was considering an offer from a businessman to build resorts in some of the mountains that surrounded Bjornland. I'm not entirely opposed to development, Latika, you should understand. I'm a businessman in my heart, possibly more than I've ever been a prince. But the proposed plans were grotesque, and the footprint would have been disastrous on the natural wilderness. I went to my father with the proposed plans. That the resorts be put on a side of the country that had mountains already developed, and that we preserve a wilderness area for future generations. He... He did not agree. I reminded him that there were a few skeletons in his closet he would not like to be revealed. He wasn't happy with that. Wasn't happy with the realization that I had ammunition to lobby at him. But there was nothing he could do. So, that's how the preserve came to be. And so it remains. Astrid has expanded those protections. And, it is something that I have made an area of expertise. How we might continue to develop in the world in a smarter, more responsible way. We must live here on this planet. Why should we not live on it more gently?"

"Says a man with a private jet?"

A rueful smile curved his lips. "That was such a predictable statement, Latika, it was nearly boring."

"Then don't be a stereotype," she said.

"I didn't say I was a paragon of any sort of virtue. Simply that I care. And I attempt to affect change in the ways I do care. As humans what else can we do? We can talk about the things that concern us, but if we have the resources to change them and we never do… Better to never even pretend that we care."

She had nothing flippant to say to that. "It's been so long since I've been able to care about anything but myself. It's exhausting."

He frowned. "I have never been given to the impression that you are selfish."

"I am," she said. "The past three years of my life has been entirely devoted to avoiding detection. It doesn't mean that I don't care about Astrid. I always have. But beneath all of it, has been concern for myself. I've had to be wrapped up in the concerns of my own survival all this time. I look forward to being able to care about something else."

She had been so mired in the idea that marrying Gunnar was to submit herself to another version of captivity that she hadn't seen it from that angle. But hearing Gunnar talking about caring for bigger things brought the reality of her own existence sharply to life. It had become closed. It had become small and mean, of necessity and that wasn't the life she wanted.

"Are you hungry?"

She blinked. "My body has no idea what time it is. I think I might be hungry. I might be exhausted. Or ready to run a marathon."

"I find the best thing to do with jet lag is to just start

eating, and keep eating so that you don't fall asleep before you are supposed to. Difficult to go to sleep while chewing steak."

She laughed. "I suppose it would be."

"Come," he said. "And let us return to my house."

CHAPTER EIGHT

GUNNAR KNEW THAT his home was impressive.

A feat of architecture. Made entirely of recycled woods and metals, and constructed into the natural shape of the mountain it was built into. He took for granted the effortless beauty of the place.

But Latika's expression of awe when they pulled up to the house forced him to look at it with new eyes. It created in him a strange sense of pride that was almost entirely unfamiliar.

He had instructed his staff to be absent upon their arrival, and to have dinner laid out and waiting. He was not disappointed, he never was. For he had learned early on that if he surrounded himself with people who thrived on the same level of excellence that he did, then everyone could exist happily.

Every member of his staff had to be almost as type A as he was. Those with less intense personality types would be miserable working for him anyway. And he found, oddly, that surrounding himself with people who had similar levels of intensity created a more serene work environment. Everyone bumped along nicely, no one impeding the progress of anyone else. Gunnar had gone and dressed for dinner, a white shirt and a pair of black pants, and he had asked Latika to do the same. Much like dinner, clothing had been laid out in advance already as well.

Some of her own things had been packed when they had left Bjornland, but he had also taken the liberty of having Astrid's stylist procure some new items.

He had expected the spread set out for them on the expansive terrace that overlooked the ocean to be perfect. And he had expected Latika to look beautiful. She always did. But he had not expected the site of her walking out of the house, wearing a dress that exposed her shapely, brown legs, and showed off her body in a way that would make any man fall to his knees and worship, to leave him utterly breathless.

He had been with some of the most beautiful women in the world. He considered his palate somewhat jaded.

But he had never been with Latika.

And suddenly, that truth felt like too heavy a thing to endure. He wanted her. With ferocity, he wanted her. There was something to her that went beyond beauty. It shimmered across her skin, captured him by the throat, with each shift and slide of that glossy black hair that hung down past her shoulder.

The dress was red. But that didn't matter. Because it *covered* her. Obscured her from his view, and that made it an irritation, rather than anything of note. She seemed oblivious to the fact that she had stunned him completely. That she had reached down inside of him and rearranged things within him so that he could not find his balance.

Like walking into a familiar room and finding the furniture somewhere unexpected.

"This really is quite lovely," she said, crossing the place.

He moved, pulling her chair out for her.

She lifted a brow. "Aren't you the perfect gentleman?"

He chuckled. "I should think a rather imperfect one."

"Perhaps." She pondered that for a moment. "Yes, you do like that story."

"It is isn't a story. It's true. The fact that I put work into a nature preserve, and give a damn about the future of the planet doesn't change these other things about me."

"I suppose not," she said.

"Does it make you feel better to imagine you might be married to someone a bit more decent then you initially thought? After all, ours is not a romantic entanglement. Is it just that you feel the need to have good feelings about partnerships?"

"No," she said. "It's because I find this version of you slightly more interesting."

"Well, I do live to be of interest to you." The words felt true. And he couldn't figure out why, when he'd meant them to be dry.

"I want to know the story," she said. "Because I can't quite piece together all these things I know about you and make one picture. I don't quite understand. I would like to."

"Why?"

"Because from the first moment I met you I... I felt drawn to you. I could not figure out why. I think the answer is in this, and I want the answer."

"Because it damages you so much to think that you want a man you don't like?"

"Maybe," she said. "But I'd like to think it's more complex than that."

"It probably isn't. We people are not overly complex. We want peace. And that's hard to come by, so when we can't find that, we chase oblivion. Through drink. Through drugs. Sex. Our bodies are inclined toward that which is a natural stimulant to us. Oftentimes emotion is separate entirely from that. People will sacrifice whole lives they've built on the offer of being entertained for a few hours. Why should you imagine you're above that?"

"Mostly because I'd like to think I don't even see a carnival ride or a glass of whiskey."

"If you have concerns about that, make it for your own sensibilities, not mine. I for one am completely comfortable being a ride for you."

"Even a ride came into being somehow. Everything was built, Gunnar, even you. And as much as you like to pretend that isn't so, as much as you like to pretend there is no authenticity in you, we both know it isn't true."

"My story is altogether uninteresting. I'm nothing more than a pampered prince, after all."

"If that's what you need me to believe."

It was the boredom in her voice that bothered him. And as they ate their meal, looking out at the ocean beyond, he did his best not to brood on it. It didn't matter whether Latika thought him interesting. He was beyond caring what other people thought, and that included her. They ate in relative silence, and he endeavored to not think overmuch about it.

"It's a strange thing," she said softly. "Growing up in a gilded cage. I understand that better than most. I was nothing but a pawn to my parents. The means by which they could gain some kind of power. I always suspected they weren't able to have more children. Because if they had a son, I think they would have been happy. Except… Maybe not. Because a daughter is an interesting pawn to use to gain greater leverage. Nobility, that was their aim. A daughter is much more useful in that sense."

"I have never thought of it that way, but I imagine so. My own father would have likely been much happier if he could have used me as a ruler, and my sister to consolidate power."

"Of course," Latika said. "My parents' greatest goal was to marry me off to someone like you. They poured every resource into me. Into making me beautiful. Into making me sophisticated. They gave me lessons. I play the piano, you know. And am minorly accomplished in ballet. I learned everything there was to know. Not so much that I would be too smart for whatever man they put me in front of, but just enough that I might be able to carry on a conversation seamlessly. That was very important to them. But none of it was about enriching me. It was all about making me into the prettiest of pets."

Gunnar's lip curled. "Like being sent to obedience training."

The idea of Latika being used in that way appalled him.

She continued. "And I understand that so many people on this earth have it worse. That they must worry about their daily survival. In terms of when they might eat again. How they can find shelter. But for so long I was a creation of my parents, and then I spent all those years in hiding. I understand. I understand that you can be surrounded by the greatest beauty in the world, by all the things that money can buy. But if the people around you only want to use you...it's empty."

"Yes, well," he said, "That is very unusual. A couple of poor little rich kids who feel assaulted by their privileged pasts. Actually, that's most dinner parties that I go to on a given day."

He regretted the words as soon as he spoke them, because Latika had been sincere. Sincerity was not something he had a great deal of experience with and it showed here. It made him deeply uncomfortable, her sharing with him. He had given her nothing and yet, she shared things that had wounded her.

But as far as he could see, it wouldn't benefit anyone for him to get into an in-depth discussion of his past.

On the other hand, there was also no reason not to.

He knew why he didn't tell Astrid. She didn't want his sister bearing any measure of burden over the things their father had done to him. But even more so, he didn't want her wounded by the knowledge of just how drastic the measures her father had been willing to take were. She knew that he had opposed her. But, all that their father had ever let Astrid see was vague disapproval. He had set up a council to obstruct her, and that had been an inconvenience. She had certainly felt the sting, the lack of their father's trust. But she didn't know the more sinister elements of his opposition.

And he never wanted her to.

There was no reason to spare Latika from the truth. And indeed, Gunnar was a resilient man. One who might bear some scars on his body, but was otherwise fine in his soul. Such as it was.

"How much has my sister told you about our father?"

"I know that he was opposed to her being the heir. But also that there was nothing he could do."

"Much of that was due to our mother," Gunnar said. "Our mother was a strong-willed woman. I always wondered why she married him. So, I suppose the title speaks for itself. Our mother made it impossible for him to simply install me onto the throne, as much as he would have liked that. Our mother made it known the world over within ten minutes of our birth that it was my sister who was the rightful heir."

"Would you have wanted to be the heir?"

"I would have done it," Gunnar said. "Anyone who wants such a mantle should not have it in the first place."

"That is probably very true."

"The weight of the crown is heavy. And Astrid's crown twice that of what many people in her position would experience. She had to be absolutely perfect. Perfect in a way that I would not have been expected to be. No, I have never envied her. Neither have I resented her. My father wished that I would. My sister's view of things was that our father favored me, but it could not be further from the truth. I am my father's biggest disappointment. What he wished for, more than anything else was for a son who craved power with the kind of avarice that he did. He wanted a son who could be trained to desire power above all else."

He watched as her face shifted, a softness to her dark eyes that he'd never seen directed at him. "But what my father never understood was the bond that twins share. My sister is a part of me. I would die for her. I would no more betray her than myself. For me, it would be impossible. When he found that he could not simply suggest that to me, he tried to force a change of heart.

He tried with everything in him. There is a dungeon in the palace, if you didn't know. And my father was not above making use of it."

Latika's face contorted. "Gunnar…"

"If I tell you this, you must promise me you will not speak of it to my sister."

"Astrid is my best friend…"

"It doesn't matter," he said. "I'm your husband. And if what you desire is intimate knowledge of my secrets, then you must understand why I have kept them."

"I want to know," she said.

"And if you want to protect Astrid, you will swear to me that she will never know."

"I swear it," Latika said, her voice a hushed whisper.

He knew there was dessert in the kitchen, but he decided to leave that bit of information. No matter how good the Princess cake, it would not be good with this story. It would likely curdle soon.

"My father didn't just doubt my sister's ability to rule. He actively despised that she would. For my father, the monarchy and the patriarchy went hand in hand. He wanted me to be his successor. But he knew that he couldn't simply demand it. First of all, we have a government in Bjornland. A council. And while that council was very loyal to my father, while they would certainly have enforced his rule in normal circumstances, the outright replacement of an heir would have been unprecedented, and indeed, would have likely been impossible without inciting some sort of civil war. When the heir to the throne is born, the military swears their allegiance. Their allegiance to the heir is equal to that of the King. It is the same with the council."

"So…"

"Short of killing my sister there was nothing he could do," Gunnar said.

"He would never have done that," Latika said, the horror laced through her tone so pure it made him feel all manner of soft things for her. He wanted to protect her from this too.

"I don't know," Gunnar responded. "But, he didn't. So, I don't know how much of that was out of the grace and goodness of his heart, and how much of that was a desire to never tarnish his legacy. You see, that was what it was all about. The desire to install me as heir was all about the perfect articulation of his legacy. To be caught murdering his own child..."

"I can't believe it," Latika said.

"Because you didn't know my father. But of course, he knew that I would have just as difficult a time taking the throne by force. But he thought that I might be able to...persuade my sister to step down. He began to educate me, as a boy, about the facts of life. He tried to instill in me an idea that women were weak. That a female ruler could never be as strong as a male counterpart. But I knew my sister. I knew my mother. While my mother wasn't perfect, her strength was unsurpassed. That is not up for debate. I can see all around me evidence that what my father said wasn't true. Astrid surpassed me in patience, and kindness. And to me, those things are a particular form of strength. One that has no sense of being threatened. Astrid is, and always will be, to my mind the rightful ruler of our nation. And nothing my father said could make me turn against her. And that was when he decided to try other methods."

"How could he possibly think he would get away with this? He wouldn't come after your sister... You..."

"Yes, he came for me. He would lock me in the dungeon for days at a time. And he would try to get me to say that I was superior. That the country would be better off with me. And I refused. What he did... It had the opposite effect. The decision that I made down in that dungeon was that I would never be manipulated. I swore my allegiance to my sister over and over again in my head, and out loud when my father came. I refused to allow him space in my head."

Gunnar could no longer look at Latika as he continued. "He didn't deserve it. And if I was truly so strong as he kept insisting I was... Well then. I felt that I should show it. Because if I had any piece of a true leader inside of me, then there should be no man on earth who can tell me what. Ironically, it was in opposing him that I found my sense of strength. And then, eventually I was no longer a boy, but closer to being a man, and my father knew that his ability to harm me, his ability to overpower me had come to an end."

"All of this happened when you were a boy?"

"Yes. That is how...bullies like to behave. Is that not what they say?"

"Gunnar," she said. "How did you survive?"

"I had purpose. My purpose was to protect Astrid."

"And then in order to flaunt your freedom from your father you... That's how you became you."

"I took great joy in forcing him to question all that he thought about who his heir should be, and how the country should be run. I took great joy in proving to him that the fact I was born a boy did not make me more suitable than my sister. Rather than her being the real thorn in his side for the rest of his days, I like to think that it was me. Solidifying to the people of the country that Astrid was the clear and rightful heir. By the time Astrid ascended the throne, I daresay there was not a single person in the entire country that wished I were their King. Do not mistake me. I don't think my sister needed my bad example to shine. But…"

"The world is a harsh and old-fashioned place," Latika said. "You don't have to tell me what it's like, you don't have to."

"So there you have it. My origin story. I'm basically a superhero movie."

Latika took a breath, and then she rose up from her seat at the table. And before Gunnar knew what was happening, she dropped to her knees before him, taking his hands in hers. "I don't know what to say."

"Don't get on your knees before me unless you intend to do something of interest with your mouth," he said, his knee-jerk reaction to seeing her sympathy.

As if taking it up as a calling, Latika stood, bending at the waist and grabbing hold of his chin. Then she closed the distance between them, and kissed him.

CHAPTER NINE

LATIKA THOUGHT THAT she might be crazy. Because this emotion and fire running through her blood was something she had never dealt with before. Because it was something that was foreign to her. Utterly and completely foreign. And yet familiar all at the same time.

Gunnar.

She wanted to touch him. She wanted to reach him. Wanted to pour all of her feelings out into his body.

For that boy that he was. That boy who must've been so terrified. Who resisted every attempt at being indoctrinated.

For the man he'd become. Arrogant and exasperating and so utterly brilliant.

She had known that he was strong, but she had only ever seen it in his irreverence. She saw now that it was his shield. That he had used it to protect himself from a Machiavellian father who had perhaps taken more joy in the attempted manipulation of his children than he cared for the outcome.

And Gunnar had kept it to himself. He had hidden it from Astrid so that she would never know the pain he endured on her behalf.

So she would be spared the full brunt of knowing her father's hatred.

The Playboy Prince was not the disgrace of the royal family of Bjornland. He was the crown jewel.

Latika had disdained him from the moment she had met him, but she had wanted him.

And she had been wrong. So utterly and completely wrong.

The man had been tortured by his father.

She kissed him deeper, allowing her thoughts to fall away. Allowing nothing more than the physical home of desire to exist between them. Gunnar growled, pulling her onto his lap.

His hold was strong, his kiss turning desperate. It was deep and intense, his tongue sliding against hers, his whiskers resting against her cheek.

Her Viking marauder who seemed intent on claiming her. No matter that she was the one who had started the kiss.

But that was all right.

If he needed to be the one to stake the claim, she could allow that. She could be that for him.

What she'd said to him had been true. She had gone without sex for twenty-four years. And in this moment, it became clear that what she had been waiting for was this. Not him specifically, but this feeling. For desire to be tattooed on every beat of her heart. For it to be an undeniable, brilliant force that she could not and did not want to deny.

"I want to see you here," he growled.

"I want to…"

"No," he said. "I have a fantasy of you," he said, standing up from the chair, holding on to her. She wrapped her legs around his waist to keep herself from sliding onto the ground. And then he walked her over to the wall and braced her back against it.

She could see him, his eyes a brilliant blue, the same as the sea behind him. Then he lifted her. Lifted her up and maneuvered her so that her thighs were over his shoulders, the wall bracing her up right.

She gasped.

He chuckled.

Then put his face directly between her thighs, with only a thin scrap of underwear keeping him from seeing everything. He held her fast with his arm, and tilted his head, kissing her inner thigh, and then he pushed her dress upward, the fabric bunching around her hips, first on one side and then the other.

"These," he said, "are very pretty." He dragged the back of his knuckle over her crease, and she squirmed. "Pity." Then he gripped the center of her panties and tugged hard, tearing the fabric. It fell free, exposing her to him, and to the open air.

"The beauty of living up on a hill like this," he said, "is that while we have a great view of all this, no one has a view of us. Latika," he whispered, pressing a kiss even higher to her inner thigh. "Latika." Then he turned his head, his tongue painting a hot stripe of pleasure over her flesh as he tasted her, deep and intense.

She gasped, letting her head fall back. She did not know how they had gotten here. With her comforting him only a moment ago, and now with him licking her in her most intimate place up against a wall. He was so big, his shoulders so broad, one large hand bracing her, holding her ass, and the other teasing her as he continued to lavish attention on her with his mouth. He made her feel small, feminine and delicate.

And most important of all, he made her feel wild.

She hadn't known. Oh, she had realized there was something hot and magical that simmered between them. Something dark and rich and unknowable. But she hadn't known that it would feel like this.

No, she'd had no idea.

She hadn't known that anything could be like this. She arched against him as he continued to lick his way to her center, as he moved his hand, sliding one finger inside of her. She gasped, rolling her hips forward, pleasure crashing over her like a wave. A precursor of something that felt like it would be bigger. Deeper.

She was desperate for something to hold onto. She put one hand on the back of his head, pushing her fingers through his blond hair, and gripped his broad, muscular shoulder with the other.

And he continued to eat her like she was dessert.

Continued to tease and torment her with that finger buried deep inside of her. One that became two, the rhythm becoming so slick and beautiful and perfect that she could barely breathe.

And then it hit. Her pleasure breaking her in half. She squeezed her legs together, rolling her hips forward and pushing his head toward her as she rode out the intense peak pleasure. And then she relaxed, letting her head fall back, releasing her hold on him. Then she realized the only thing keeping her from falling down to the earth was the fact that he was holding onto her. He lifted her easily from his shoulders and pulled her into his arms. "You are beyond anything I could have guessed you might be," he said, his voice rough.

"So are you," she said, feeling dizzy.

"I want you," he said. "More than I can remember wanting anything. When I was down in that dungeon I used to think of things that I like. Cars. Cake. My desires were simple then. Moving into adolescence, I thought an awful lot about women. I would picture things I wanted and couldn't have over and over again."

His words were rough. Compelling. Like he was touching her. Over her body. In her body. She was on fire.

"A study in perfect, torturous deprivation," he continued. "And once I got my freedom I never wanted for anything again. I wouldn't allow it. I indulged in everything. Until you. You… I wanted you from the moment I first saw you. And you made me wait. Oh, Latika you don't even know what a sin that is. To a man like me…"

"Have me," she said, her whole body electric with want.

He could. He could have her. Out here if he wanted to. Against the wall. On the floor. Whatever he wanted, he could have. Whatever he needed, she would become. For him, she would do anything.

He growled, picking her up and sweeping her into his arms, blazing a path into the house. He left the door open behind them, but it was clear that he felt secure and isolated up here in his house on the top of the mountain. He carried her up the stairs, and she barely had the chance to take in the beauty before her.

All the clean lines, warm, honey-colored wood panels and open, sun-drenched vistas provided by the windows that overtook each and every wall.

They went up three flights of stairs, to a bedroom that was positioned higher than the rest of the house, built into the side of the hill, made entirely of windows that looked out over the sea that faded from jade to deepest navy. White-capped waves swelled reaching up toward the sky that was open and like the desire the swelling inside of Latika.

So soon.

So *impossibly* soon after the peak he had just brought her to. The bed itself was large, white and spare, upon a raised platform that put it in line with the view below.

And it loomed larger still, as he carried Latika to it, setting her down on the plush surface.

He laid her down on her back, and she blushed when she realized that her legs had fallen open, and that she was still naked beneath her dress.

"Too late for modesty," he said, pushing his hand against her knee and holding her legs open before she could close them.

Then he moved up her body, reaching around behind her and undoing the zipper on the little red dress that had barely gotten an hour's worth of wear. He pulled down, exposing the bra she was wearing beneath. Lacy and insubstantial, with gaps between the intricate flower design, giving him a clear view of the shape of her nipples.

She knew. Because she had put it on and looked in the mirror and wondered what he might think.

Those eyes became a blue flame, the desire in them so clear, so potent, that she didn't have to wonder.

He wanted her. She had been so focused on wanting to make him feel good that she hadn't fully realized what a wonderful thing it was for her to be wanted by him.

No one had ever wanted her. Not her, as she was.

They wanted her to be the perfect daughter and representation of all that they were. Wanted her to be a perfect prisoner and a slave.

She had been the daughter. A fugitive. An assistant.

Never just a woman. And now, with Gunnar's hungry gaze roaming over her curves, woman was exactly what she became. What she felt, straight down to her soul. He pulled the dress the rest of the way from her body and cast it onto the floor.

Then he moved back to her, unhooking her bra and sending it the same direction as the dress. She still had her shoes on, and it should feel ridiculous, her knees bent, her elbows propping her up, her black hair cascading over her body like a wave.

Like she was a pinup, and not a virgin about to surrender to a man with more experience than she could possibly imagine.

But whether she was Madonna or siren, Gunnar didn't seem to mind. He growled, lowering his head and pressing a kiss to her neck, nibbling his way to her jaw, and to her lips, where he treated her to kiss after drugging kiss, ecstasy making her limbs feel heavy.

Then he tore himself away from her mouth again, making his way down, kissing the delicate skin around her breasts, knee, before moving up to suck her nipple.

She gasped, shocked at the arrow of pleasure that pierced her, so deep and so true she wouldn't have thought that she could feel such pleasure again. Not so close to what he had given her release before.

But still she felt it. And it left her utterly transfixed, in desperate need of more.

"You," she murmured even as he moved over to her

other breast, licking and sucking, bringing her nipple into its heightened point. "I need you."

He stood, and began to unbutton his shirt, letting it fall open, revealing that beautiful body she had admired so many times. Those perfect muscles, dusted with just the right amount of hair.

And then he moved his hands to his belt, and her throat went dry. This was the part of him that remained a mystery to her, and the very idea of seeing him now sent little rivulets of pleasure straight through her.

She wanted him.

Wanted *this*.

He pushed his hands down, along with his underwear, and her breath left her body. He was beautiful. Every inch of him.

And there were a great many inches.

No wonder women lost their minds over this man.

He was everything a man should be. Large and broad and thick all over. The most stunning sight she ever beheld. He was art.

A man seemingly carved from marble and made into hot, delicious flesh.

"See anything you like?" His lips tipped upward, that indolent smile she knew so well curving that wicked mouth.

"Just you," she said, breathless. "That's all."

He growled, coming down onto the bed with her, every inch of his naked body touching every inch of hers. She rolled against him, desperately needy.

He kissed her.

Kissed her until she was slick with her need for him. Kissed her until she felt hollow. Until she thought she might die of the need to have him inside of her. He wrapped his hand around his heavy length, pressing the head to the entrance of her body, then drawing the moisture from inside of her and up the sensitive bundle of nerves at the apex of her thighs.

He teased her like that, teased them both, slowly, sensually, the pleasure like a lightning strike as he did. When finally placed that thick head back in her entrance, she was trembling. Ready to make him come inside of her.

She might not know if it would hurt, and exactly what it would feel like, but she knew it was what she needed. Knew that only this would bring the fulfillment that she craved.

He rocked his hips forward, and she gasped when he reached the much discussed hymen, but he didn't seem to notice, as he rolled his hips forward, filling her completely.

It hurt, but only for a moment. And then it was nothing but a sense of completion. Of desire deep and real, as her internal muscles gripped him and seemed to pull him deeper inside.

She rocked her hips against his body, and it was like gasoline thrown onto a lit match. They combusted. His thrusts were wild, and seeing him like this, feral and without that urbane wit that he used as a shield between himself and the world, seeing him pure and unguarded, his teeth bared like an animal, his ice blue eyes hot and fierce, his entire body reverberating with a growl every time he claimed her body with his own, was the most intoxicating aphrodisiac that Latika could have ever fathomed. She'd never known how wonderful it could be to be desired by a man.

No. Not by a man.

By *this* man.

This man was everything.

He thrust home, grinding his hips against hers, release bursting overhead like fireworks. And then on a growl, he seemed to give up his control, his big body shook as his length pulsed inside of her, as he spilled himself into her.

And then they lay together, breathing hard, slick with sweat, and all tangled up in each other. Then he moved away from her, with shocking speed and the fluid grace of a panther.

"You were a virgin," he said.

She rolled to the side, revealing a spot of blood, shame filling her. "Yes," she said.

"Then tell me, Latika. You don't happen to be taking the pill, do you?"

And that was when she realized, that she and Gunnar did not use protection.

And given the timing of the month, the risk of her getting pregnant was very real.

Gunnar's pulse was hammering wildly out of control. "Are you on anything?" he repeated.

"No," she answered. The answer that he knew she would give. Rage spiraled through his veins.

"I told you that I never want to have children."

"I wasn't thinking," she said, her face getting pale. "I…"

"I don't believe you," he said, rage an unforgiving, unreasonable monster in his gut.

And when he got down past that bright, burning rage, there was something far worse under it. A sense that he had to escape his skin. That his body, his very essence, had betrayed him and there was no fixing it.

Things had been set into motion that could now not be stopped and the absolute terror he felt over that...

Over the possibility of fatherhood.

He couldn't breathe.

"I don't care what you believe," Latika said. "I didn't think of it. You clearly didn't either, so I don't know why I should be the focus of your rage."

"Is there a pill you can take?" There had to be something. A way to turn back the clock. To stop the mistake.

Her expression contorted. Shock. To pain. To rage. "I refuse," she said. "What will be will be, the mistake was ours, and I'm not going to reverse course and make a decision that I will personally regret."

"Because you want a baby," he said. "And that was your goal along."

She frowned. "No. I do want to have a baby. I always have. But to act as if I was somehow using my feminine wiles to manipulate you..." She stood up, hunting for her dress. "There are easier ways to get sperm, Gunnar. Every single one of them involves not having to put up with you."

"Yet, producing a child with me comes as a very hefty reward, I should think."

"I married you already," she snapped. "Where's the benefit of manipulating you? How would that get me money I don't already have access to?"

He knew that what she was saying was true, and that his response was unreasonable. And yet, he could not stop himself. Panic was overtaking him now, and it was an emotion he was not familiar with.

He had spent days locked in a dungeon in the castle

in Bjornland, and not felt panic. He did not know who he was, and if he despised her for anything, it was this most of all.

He felt like his skin was not his own, and that was something that could not be endured.

"I will have nothing to do with the child," he said.

He expected the words to bring with them a rush of relief. Because it was a decision, if nothing else, and it was the unknown that he could not bear above all else.

But he felt no relief. Instead, all he felt was a sick kind of grim determination that settled low in his stomach and refused to be moved.

"You won't have anything to do with your own child?"

"I already told you how things would be. You are the one who refuses to be reasonable here."

"Fine. Then you may have nothing to do with the child. But if there is a child, and that is your stance, you will have nothing to do with me either. You wanted me. You had me. Understand that it is the last time."

"That's it then? Your first time will be your last?"

She whirled around, her eyes a glittering brown blaze. "It will not be my last. I will go about my life as if I do not have a husband who would deny his own child. I will be discreet, but trust that I will find someone who will share my life with me. And if you seek to cast me out, then the world will know of your cruelty. If Ragnar comes and scoops me up because you deny me your protection, when I have your child, then what will the world think of you? And isn't that why you're doing this? So the world will think better of you. I thought... I thought beneath it all was a good man. But no. You're a bad man, Gunnar. And just because you did something good for your sister doesn't erase that."

Fury rose up inside of him and he reached out, grabbing hold of her arm. "Don't you think I know that? Don't you think I already know that I'm dark beyond the telling of it? It doesn't matter how much light I throw onto myself, doesn't matter how much I pretend to be a man filled with nothing but cares for where his next drink might come from, that I don't know that my soul is a pit."

He released his hold on her.

"Even if there is no child, you will not touch me," she said. "I could never be with a man who would say the things that you have. Who thinks the way that you do. I'm appalled by you. Disgusted. As much as I ever wanted you. I'm going to shower now. I need to wash you off of me."

She turned and went into the shower, and he let her go.

He prowled down the hall, pacing back and forth, and then he went into his office. He looked out over the ocean. He would have liked to stay here longer, but their time here was at an end. He had accomplished what he had come for. They had made a show of his company. Had revealed what a fantastically generous soul he was. But he was more than he had always shown the public.

And he had revealed to Latika just how broken he was.

All the sharp edges that lived inside of him that would only cut those who dared come closest to him.

It was time to leave.

He made a phone call to his pilot. "Ready the plane. We depart first thing in the morning."

CHAPTER TEN

THE TRIP BACK to Bjornland was worse than the trip to the States. Latika was reeling from the speed at which they had boomeranged between one continent and another. And if the bed had been uncomfortable and awkward, looming large on the plane on the way over, it was worse now.

Worse now that she had been with him. Worse now she knew all the things he could make her feel in a bed like that.

She felt sick with regret. With sadness.

Because she had felt... For one fleeting moment she had thought maybe she'd found love.

Oh, she wasn't so foolish to think that Gunnar would have immediately fallen in love with her, just because he had bared his soul. But she had felt something for him. Something that had surpassed anything. As if he was what her heart had been waiting for all along. And then it had been for nothing.

Because he had revealed the truth of himself.

He would ignore their child, would hold himself separate. Would sleep with her, and disavow a life they had created.

And she could not endure that. She could not set a child up for that kind of pain.

Nor herself.

She felt sick with worry. Sick with regret.

When they finally arrived in Bjornland, they did not go to the palace, but to Gunnar's apartments.

She didn't know why that surprised her.

"We will be living here," he said. "Your things have already been moved."

"Of course," she said, feeling like she was floating outside of her body.

On numb feet she walked into the bedroom that he had gestured toward. All her things were there. And it was separate from his.

That was a good thing. Because the only thing she could see happening now was the two of them living separate lives.

In this space that was so much smaller than the palace.

She flung herself down onto the bed, and she couldn't cry. Instead she just lay there with eyes that felt like they had been rubbed with sand.

The next week was a blur, the days leading together like strokes of watercolor on a page.

Except they weren't blurry, no. Latika was all too tied in with what was happening in her life.

And worst of all the things she hadn't fully thought through, she was not Astrid's assistant anymore.

She was robbed of the thing that used to keep her occupied. And robbed of an excuse to spend time with her best friend.

On the fourth day since they returned home, Astrid called her.

"You know, it's quite ridiculous that you're acting as if we can't spend time together simply because you don't work for me anymore."

The truth of the matter was, Latika was partly avoiding Astrid, because she didn't want her friend to notice how sad she was.

She couldn't talk to her about Gunnar's revelations, because she had promised, and because she understood why Gunnar felt that way. She agreed with him. To reveal everything would be to harm Astrid, and Latika didn't want to do that. But she was bored, and she and Gunnar hadn't spoken in days. Her husband came and went like a thief in the night, and otherwise was never home.

She wondered—with a brilliant, burning stab in her chest—if he was already in the beds of other women.

And why shouldn't he be?

Just because he'd been with her a few days earlier wouldn't keep him from seeking another lover. It never had before, not with any other woman, so why would it be different with her? He had made it plain she didn't really matter to him.

So when she had been back a week, she entered the palace for the first time since her marriage and walked slowly into Astrid's personal parlor.

"Hi," Astrid said.

"Hello," Latika responded.

"You don't look good," Astrid said.

"It's fine," Latika said.

"Is being married to my brother such a trial?"

She tried to force a smile. "I knew you would ask me about him."

"Is that why you were avoiding me?"

"No," she said slowly. "Things are strange. Things have changed. And I didn't want to assume…"

"Our friendship is more than you working for me. It's even more than you being married to my brother. I care about you because I care about you. It isn't connected to what you can do for me."

Latika was suddenly so very glad she came, because she had never needed to hear something more in her entire life. It was the thing that she had longed to hear from her parents. The thing she had been hungry for in a relationship all her life.

"Thank you," she said, with deep sincerity. "Thank you. I'm not sure anyone else has ever felt that way."

"Then the other people in your life are fools. And if my brother is one of them, so is he."

They let go of talk of Gunnar, and instead enjoyed lunch, until Astrid's phone rang. She picked it up, her brows shooting upward. "Really? You are sure. You are absolutely certain. Because if this is a hoax of some kind… No. I understand. I'll tell her."

Astrid hung up the phone and leveled her gaze at Latika. "Ragnar is dead."

And just like that, her world, that had seemed right for a moment, turned itself on its head again.

Latika waited. She waited until darkness fell. And Gunnar was still not home. Then she procured the use of his private plane, which was available to her even when she had been Astrid's assistant, and was now unquestionably available to her as his wife.

She flew to Italy. Then requested the jet be sent back home.

From there she got a ticket through a commercial airline and flew to England.

She had money in accounts there. And she knew that if he really wanted to, he could likely find her. But, it would take a little bit of time. Because she had secured her money using an alias, as she had done with her credit cards. Saving them for an emergency. For years, she had no need to spend her earnings as Astrid's assistant that she had socked away, hidden from both her parents and Ragnar.

Ragnar was dead. Something so benign as a heart attack seemed so bizarre given how things had been. But that was what had killed him.

And because Ragnar was dead she did not have to stay with Gunnar.

She booked herself into a hotel room near Piccadilly, cursing the proximity to such insanity, but also grateful for the last-minute availability.

Then she collapsed onto the bed.

And this time tears came.

And when they began to fall, she feared they wouldn't stop.

She was free now. Free from everything. But it didn't feel like freedom. It felt like nothing she would've ever wanted for herself, and for the life of her, she couldn't figure out why.

Gunnar.

She didn't want to believe it.

Didn't want to believe that a man who would say those things to her, who would reject his own child like that, could possibly be the reason she suddenly felt like she didn't want the thing she had been craving all her life.

"I have no obligation to anyone," she said into the empty room. "I am free to go where I want. To do what I want."

She waited for that truth to sink in. Waited for it to make her feel good.

It never did.

When Gunnar arrived back home in the wee hours of the morning, something felt strange in the apartment.

But he had spent the evening working at an office that he owned downtown in the capital city of Bjornland—completely unnecessarily, as he could easily work in the palace, or at home—and he was exhausted. He collapsed into bed without investigating the source of the feeling.

He woke the next morning, it persisted.

Typically, he was out until after Latika went to bed, and she was gone by the time he woke up. So the emptiness in the apartment was normal enough. He went to look at her room, and found everything as it should be. Her clothes were hanging in the closet, her shoes lined up.

But then, late that night when he came home again, he checked, and she still hadn't returned.

He called Astrid. "Do you have any idea where my wife is?"

"No," said, her voice filled with concern.

"If that bastard Ragnar..."

"Ragnar is dead," Astrid said.

"What?"

"Latika didn't tell you?"

"No. I haven't seen her. When did you discover this?"

"Early the day before yesterday. You haven't spoken to her since then?"

"I... I haven't seen her."

"Gunnar!" Astrid sounded incredulous. "You haven't seen your wife in two days, your wife has been under threat, and you didn't think to say anything about it?"

"We don't go out of our way to spend much time together," he said, his voice flat.

"I don't know what's going on between the two..."

"Nothing," Gunter said. "Nothing is going on between the two of us."

"That isn't right *when you're married.*"

"You know we didn't marry for conventional reasons."

"Have you tried calling her?" Astrid asked.

"No," he said. "But I will."

He hung up the phone, and dialed Latika's number.

She picked up on the second ring.

"Where are you?" he asked, not waiting for her to speak.

"We don't need to be together," she said, sidestepping the question.

"What the hell are you talking about?"

"Ragnar is dead. And the two of us have no reason to continue on with this farce of a marriage. I've taken myself away from you, for a reason."

"What about my reputation?"

"I'll see that it's handled," she said. "I'll see that there is no doubt that the problem was mine. That it's my fault the marriage dissolved. I will be held responsible, and your reputation will be intact. The response that has been given to you owning your corporation has been overwhelmingly positive. I think that you'll find everything will be just fine without me."

"Latika..."

The line went dead, and she didn't speak after.

Each attempt at calling her after that was met with dead air. She refused to answer. And because of that, he couldn't figure out a way to track her phone. He looked for credit cards, and could find nothing.

Any easy paper trail had been erased.

And then, two weeks after his wife had left home, her name popped up in a database. Her real name had been used at a private physician's office.

One specializing in obstetrics.

Gunnar picked up his phone. "We are going to London."

CHAPTER ELEVEN

LATIKA WAS EXHAUSTED by the time she got home. She didn't know whether to laugh or cry. Honestly, she felt like doing both.

She was pregnant.

Pregnant with Gunnar's baby.

The exact thing that would have driven their marriage to the brink anyway.

She owed Ragnar a thank you note for dying of a heart attack with such excellent timing.

She was surprised by the way he had died. Considering it never seemed as though he had a heart.

The thought made her laugh. And then she realized she was a crazy person, standing in her empty apartment, shaking and laughing. The news she had been given today was life altering. She hadn't wanted to be seen out and about purchasing a pregnancy test, nor had she seen the way she could possibly go to a public hospital.

Thankfully, she had so much money squirreled away, that it hadn't been beyond her to get herself into a private clinic.

She had worn a scarf over her head, and large sunglasses, and it felt ridiculous.

But she seemed to have pulled it off. There were no headlines proclaiming that she was in London, after all.

Incognito still was hindering her new sense of freedom. Perhaps that was why she still felt so heavy.

She was resolute in her purpose. She knew exactly what she needed to do. She only needed a few hours to get everything straight.

And a few hours was all it took. With her press release crafted, she was ready to push it out to new sources.

That her marriage to Gunnar was a sham. That she was the villain. That she had married him under false pretenses, and had later found out she was pregnant with a lover's baby.

And that she had decided to dissolve the marriage as a result.

Not him.

Gunnar, she would say, had offered to raise the child as its own.

Because when her child looked back on the news stories surrounding his or her birth, she wanted to have that child feel as if they were wanted by everyone.

Especially their father.

Even if they never knew that Gunnar was their actual father. It was sad to think that would be how it was, but it would have to be. It would be better for everyone.

And everyone would be protected. She wished desperately she could have a glass of wine with this upsetting turn of events, but she couldn't.

Because of the baby.

She smiled, pressing her hand to her stomach.

If nothing else she had purpose now. Maybe it wasn't

wild, giddy freedom. But purpose would be better. Purpose actually made her much, much happier.

She steeled herself, her finger poised to push Send on the press release. And that was when the door to the hotel room opened.

Latika turned, her mouth falling open when she saw him standing there. His expression was grim, an aura of leashed violence around him that she had never before witnessed.

Gunnar excelled in exuding laconic grace.

She had always sensed that there was the potential for danger lurking beneath that exterior. That the way he lounged about the palace in Bjornland was much like a big cat. Watching. Waiting. Incapable of striking with decisive and fatal force in the time that it would take a person to bat an eyelash.

And here it was now. Raw, unvarnished and unconcealed. How had she never seen this before? Gunnar was not a safe space.

Gunnar was lethal.

And she suspected she had crossed him in a way she had not foreseen.

"Feeling relaxed?" he asked.

"I was," she responded, standing up from the computer and stepping in front of the screen. He walked into the room, closing the door behind him.

"How did you get a key?"

He looked at her, one brow raised. He did not answer her question.

"Ragnar is dead," she said. "I had no reason to hide in Bjornland anymore. I saw the opportunity to claim my freedom, and I did it. Don't worry, I will make sure that there is no…"

"You're pregnant," he said.

Everything inside of her went still. Her heart thundered. She felt very much like a field mouse under the watchful eye of the lion. She had no hope of pulling a thorn out of his paw and making it better. For he was looking at her as if she was the one who had put it there.

"You don't want a baby," she said.

"You should've told me."

"Why? Everything is in hand."

"How dare you? How dare you flee in the night and take my heir from me."

His rage was stark. Palpable. And it took all her strength to find a way to speak with that anger, another entity in the room, pressing in on her.

"First of all," she said, "I took myself from you. I claimed my freedom. I didn't know I was pregnant when I left you. It had to do with me, not a baby. Second of all, you said unequivocally that you did not want a child. That you would have nothing to do with a child that we created."

"That is different than allowing my child to be raised away from the palace, and from its birthright."

"What birthright? You're the spare, Gunnar. Every child that Astrid has will be in line before you, and our child would never be in line at all."

"It doesn't matter. All that matters is that my child receive the rights they are entitled to by birth."

"But you don't want them. And I don't want to subject them to such a thing."

"And I will not allow this. You think that you can walk away from me? What about our bargain? You cannot step into this space and use me as a safety net and then leave when it suits you."

"If you're worried for your precious reputation, don't be." She stepped to the side, revealing her computer screen. "I am prepared to absolve you of any wrong-doing. I have prepared a press release, which I'm ready to push the button on. Wherein I declare that this child belongs to a lover that I took before our marriage, and that you offered to give my child your name, and I refused. My reputation will be in tatters, while yours will remain intact. But I don't care. I care nothing for my reputation, I never wanted notoriety. All I have ever wanted is the chance to live my life on my terms. I'm ready to go off in the country and raise this baby alone. I will be happy doing it."

It wasn't sacrifice on her end. It was the pursuit of freedom. The need to cut ties with him utterly and completely. To uphold her end of their bargain so she might walk owing him nothing.

They had married for his reputation, and for her protection.

She no longer needed protection. And if she just lowered herself, her leaving him would allow him to be blameless.

And the slate would be clean between them.

She would finally be free.

"So," he said, his tone soft. Deadly. "You seek to use me as a sperm donor?"

"Why not?" She lifted her chin up, determined to pour every ounce of defiance she possessed onto him. "Astrid sought to do the same."

"It didn't work out for her, did it?"

"Because Mauro has a heart. Because he was willing to cross borders to claim his child. You don't want yours."

"Have I not crossed borders?" he asked, throwing his arms wide. "Is this the demonstration you were hoping to see? I passed your purity test that I might be able to be father to my own flesh and blood?"

"You were the one who disavowed him," she said, advancing on him. "And in so doing, you disavowed *me*. I will not allow my child a relationship with a father that doesn't want them. If I do, how am I any different than your mother? How am I any different at all? And how are you different from your father? He didn't want Astrid. And his desire to be rid of her made him do appalling things to you. Is that what you want? Is that the place you want your child to grow up?"

He went very still. And Latika knew that she had overplayed her hand.

She had been attempting to manipulate, with a knife straight to the heart. But she could see the moment he grabbed the handle of that metaphorical knife, intent on turning it back around.

He closed the space between them, those ice blue eyes cutting her with the chill in them. He stopped when he was a breath away from her, his chest nearly touching her breasts. He leaned in, his mouth set to a grim line. And then he reached past her, grabbing her laptop and wrenching it free of the charger cord.

He threw it down onto the ground and stomped it beneath his shoe.

The screen went fuzzy, then black. Her heart thundered in abject terror, her entire body trembling.

"The child is mine. So are you. If you want to see what I'm capable of, if you want to see the ruthlessness that my father planted into my soul, then you have given yourself a perfect opportunity to do so. My people are descended of Vikings. Do you know what we do when there is something we desire, and it does not belong to us? We take it, and we make it ours. And you, make no mistake, are mine."

He grabbed hold of her, that large, commanding fist buried in her hair as he pulled her forward, his mouth crashing down on hers. She couldn't breathe. Couldn't think. She was melting, the inferno of his rage demolishing each and every one of her defenses.

She could feel it. Like a rally cry inside of her soul. *Surrender.*

She shouldn't want to surrender. It was a foolish thing to do. And it was one she could not afford. And yet, her Viking marauder would accept nothing less, and somehow her body was intent upon allowing it.

Then he picked her up, swept her straight off of her feet, and carried her into the bedroom.

CHAPTER TWELVE

GUNNAR'S RAGE WAS a living thing. Boiling over, spilling out of control.

Latika had said that he was like his father. And he couldn't find it in himself to fight the ways in which that might be true. He was failing. And yet... She was in his arms. She was clinging to him, kissing him back like liquid fire. And he could do nothing to deny himself. With blinding heat, blinding needs, pulsing behind his eyes, and hard, heady desire pulsing through him he could do nothing but stake his claim.

If it was in his blood, if it was inevitable, then he would surrender.

The bedroom in the hotel suite she was occupying had large windows, overlooking the neon and chaos of the city. It was all noise, next to the sophisticated serenity that Latika possessed. She was dressed simply today, and a black dress that hugged her luscious body, cut off just above the knee.

It was demure, really. And yet, it ignited a fire in his veins that would rival the forge of any dwarf king found in the stories his nannies had told him as a boy.

And indeed, his need was honed to a sharpened edge, like an axe. And when it fell, it would be decisive and deadly. He took her to the window, turned her so that she was facing out.

"You know how I got in here," he said. "I was handed a key. Because you are mine, and the world knows it. Everyone down there… They would not lift a finger to take you out of my custody. You are mine. The whole world knows." He gripped the zipper on her dress and pulled it down, letting it fall off of her body, and pool at her feet.

She was wearing black underwear, lace and revealing, highlighting the curves of her delicious ass. He pushed his hand beneath the waistband, grabbing a handful of soft, plump flesh. Before pushing his hand further between her thighs, feeling how wet she was.

"You desire me even now. You ran from me, and you still desire me."

"We all want things that we despise," she said.

"Do we? Or do bodies sometimes know better than our minds?"

"My heart wants nothing to do with you."

"And yet." He leaned in, toying with her between her legs. "Tell me no. If you don't want this. If you don't want me. Tell me no."

"Bastard," she spat.

"Does my touch disgust you?" He drew his fingers across that place where he knew she was most sensitive. She gasped, rolling her hips forward. "Oh, yes," he said. "I can see the way I disgust you. So much that you're on the verge of coming…out of your skin."

"Let me go," she said. "You don't want me. You don't want the baby."

"Don't tell me what I want," he said, stroking her in time with his words. "Don't speak to me like you know. Tell me what you want. Tell me if you want me to stop."

Again, she did. She simply stood, vibrating with fury and need as he stroked her. And he was filled with just enough rage over her abandonment to continue to push. "Are you afraid that if you push me too hard I'll disappear, never to return? Because you can profess to hate me all you want, because you love what I do to your body. I'm sure being a Duchess doesn't hurt."

"I don't give a damn about being your Duchess."

"But you do give a damn about pleasure, don't you? Is it wounding, to discover you're just as base as the rest of us? So many years of abstinence for you, darling Latika, only to be undone so resolutely by my touch. That must be extremely confronting for you."

"Are you going to do something? Are you going to stand there all night with your hands between my legs halfheartedly pleasuring me."

"Oh," he said. "My mistake. Did you want me to put some effort into it?"

He turned around so that she was facing him, and unhooked her bra, throwing it down to the ground, then he dragged her panties down, pressing a kiss to her ankle, her calf, her thigh before standing. Her eyes glittered with rage, her frame shaking.

"One last chance, darling. Tell me no."

Her dark eyes glittered with rage and desire. "Go to hell."

"I'll take that as an enthusiastic *yes*."

He crushed her up against his body, reveling in the feel of all that soft skin beneath his hands, while he remained fully clothed. He kissed her then, pouring all of the fury and outrage that he felt into her body. Into her soul.

If she thought he was a monster, she would get a monster.

He stripped his clothes off quickly, then lifted her up, set her down on the bed. He maneuvered her so that she was on her knees, her thighs thick and luscious, her waist slim. Her breasts heavy. He stroked himself twice, looking at the picture that she made.

"That's more like it," he said. "On your knees, showing a bit of deference to your King. But I should like a bit of praise from your mouth."

She looked up at him, the reluctant hunger on her face an aphrodisiac. He pressed the head of his masculinity to her lips and he saw the moment she surrendered to her need. Her tongue darted out, touching the tip of him and then she opened wide, taking him and as far as she could.

He grabbed hold of her hair, guiding her movements as she pleasured him. And somehow, the game they were playing got lost. Got all tangled up in the dark, deep pleasure threatening to overwhelm him.

Because he could not remember why he was angry anymore. And he could not remember why he had thought allowing her to put her lips on him would give him the power. For she held in her hand the most vulnerable part of him. And he was a slave to the need that she created, with clever fingers and lips and tongue.

He was the one surrendering.

He growled, pulling her away from him and turning her so that she was facing away. Still on her knees. He pressed himself to the entrance of her body, before thrusting deep, holding tightly to her hips as he led the deep, intense pleasure of being inside of her wash over him. She looked over her shoulder, her black hair covering part of her face, her expression one of dazed wonder.

Then, he began to move.

He lost himself in it. In that rhythm, deep and steady. And whatever he had been thinking to put her in this position, to make her so much less Latika that she was, it didn't work. For there was no other woman who felt like her. Who made him feel like this. There was nothing in all the world had ever felt like this.

Pleasure was like an arrow, piercing him, making it difficult to breathe. It was as though it had punched his lung. His heart. He put his hand between her legs and squeezed her, before moving one finger to either side of the center of her need and stroking, until a hoarse cry left her lips and her internal muscles pulsed around him. Only then did he allow the pleasure in him to rage out of control. He pulsed inside of her, pouring himself into her body, spending everything in her.

And when it was done, he collapsed at her side, laying on his back, feeling like a warrior left for dead on the battlefield.

Latika was laying on her stomach, her head turned to one side, the one visible eye appraising him closely.

"Pack your things," he said. "You're coming back to Bjornland with me."

He had embraced all that he was. He had become the conqueror. The marauder.

And yet somehow, as he headed out the door to the hotel, with Latika mutely walking beside him, he felt more the captive than the captor.

Latika could not untangle the events of the past few hours. And even when she was back in the palace in Bjornland, she felt dazed.

Gunnar had made some noise about the fact the two of them needed to be in residence at the palace for a time, but she hadn't fully understood why. For what all the implications might be. He had their things moved into the same bedroom, and Latika knew that everything between them would be different now. And not necessarily for the better. The way that he had broken that laptop so decisively, and then claimed her body with such force replayed in her mind over and over.

He had left impressions on her and in her that were so deep she could still feel them reverberating within her hours later.

She could not pretend that she hadn't been a willing participant. Could not pretend that part of her hadn't been thrilled that he had come for her.

That he had done exactly what Mauro had done for Astrid, for their child. Crossed borders and made demands.

But she still didn't get the sense that Gunnar wanted their child out of a sense other than…she couldn't even fathom what he was doing.

There was a sense of obligation, that she knew, but it didn't come from a place of love. Not remotely. Either way, it didn't matter. She was here. He had given her a great many opportunities to turn him away, and she had not. However she might regret it now, however she might feel weaker for it now, the choice had been hers. A strange realization. She had choice. She had given it to him.

"You're back," Astrid said, walking with great purpose into Gunnar's living quarters.

"Yes," Latika said.

"Why did you leave?"

"Because Ragnar was dead. And I didn't need to stay."

"But you're back," Astrid pointed out.

Latika knew that she couldn't keep any of this from her friend. There was no real point to it. She would find out eventually.

She only wished that there was some way she could sidestep the fact that of course she and Gunnar had ended up in a sexual relationship. Mostly because she didn't want to sit there and have to bear Astrid being right.

She was raw enough without having to admit that she had been wrong about her own desires.

"Gunnar, for his part, did not think that it was a good time to dissolve our marriage," Latika said.

"Did he not?" Astrid's tone sounded light, casual and wholly unsurprised.

"No," she said, knowing that she was being less than forthcoming.

"And why is that?"

"Perhaps because I'm pregnant," she said crisply.

That succeeded in shocking Astrid into silence. But, Latika could scarcely enjoy that.

"Did you know that when you left?" she asked.

"No," she said defensively. Though, it wouldn't have made a difference in her actions. Not after all that he'd said.

"You said my brother didn't want children."

"He doesn't. And he's quite angry with me. But I seem to recall he was involved in forgetting to use protection."

Astrid grimaced. But then, her expression softened. "I seem to recall having to cope with a very angry man who seems to think that a lack of protection was entirely my fault."

"Amazing creatures, men," Latika said. "Are they not?"

"They are something," Astrid agreed.

"So you're staying married?"

"For the time being," Latika said. Then she sighed. "He does not love me."

"Do you love him?"

She thought about it. For good while. All that he told her about his relationship with his father... It made her feel things for him. But then... There was the way he was acting about this child. All the things he had said. But then, the way he behaved as well. It was difficult to sort out what was true. And it was very hard for her to figure out her response.

"He doesn't want our baby. But he also doesn't want to let it go. I find... I don't know how I can love a man who will not love his child."

Astrid nodded gravely. "Give him time. And a chance to change."

"Some men never do," she said, thinking of their father.

"No," she said. "Some men never do."

"And if he doesn't?" Latika asked.

"Then I will be first in line to help set you free. But barring anything egregious... I think the two of you need to work this out for yourselves."

And as much as Latika would like to disagree, she couldn't. Because she might have been forced into the marriage mess, but no one had forced her into his bed. Twice. She was responsible for her own part in this. And she would not pawn that responsibility off. No matter how difficult it was. And right now, it was all pretty damn stiff.

* * *

Women had never made Gunnar nervous. He was a man who had a certain effect on the fairer sex, and he was well aware of that fact. He had always enjoyed the sort of attention he'd received in that regard. But he was walking on uneven ground with Latika. He felt off balance and out of his depth. He disliked that greatly. "Did you have a good day?" he asked.

"Yes," she responded.

"What did you do?"

"I spent some time with Astrid."

"And?"

"And we had a nice time," she said. "But I always do with your sister."

"Good."

She said nothing. Instead, she began to move about the room, ignoring him pointedly as she sifted through drawers in the large, ornate armoire at the back wall.

"What are you looking for?"

"Something to sleep in," she said.

"I certainly don't require that you wear anything to bed."

She looked at him, her expression verging on incredulous. "Do you expect that I'm going to have sex with you?"

He had. He had very much expected that. After all, she had seemed fully and completely into his body when he had encountered her that morning.

It had only been that morning.

It seemed an eternity now.

"It's no secret that you're attracted to me," he said.

"It's no secret that you have rejected our child. That's why I left. No, I didn't know I was pregnant, but I could not abide the idea of being married to a man who would see a child the way that you do."

"Things are different now that it's a reality," he said, believing that the moment the words left his lips.

"In what way?"

"In the sense that I understand deeply that I have an obligation to this child. And I intend to fulfill that obligation."

"A child should be more than an obligation. Just as a child should be more than a means to an end for an avaricious father intent on having his will be done through his descendants. You should love a child."

"I understand loyalty," he said. "I'm not certain that I understand love."

The look on Latika's face was what made him realize that there was something heavy in those words. Something shocking and wrong. He'd always known that to be true about himself. That he didn't understand that kind of depth.

He had been forced to exist in dark, enclosed spaces and he'd grown armor to protect himself. But it had cost. Because all those layers he'd built up had smothered a flame inside of him.

Or maybe…maybe that flame that existed inside other people had never been in him.

"What about Astrid?"

"You are the one who accused me of not caring for my sister, and now you seek to hold her up as an example of how I do?"

"No I… I'm sorry. I never should have implied that you didn't love Astrid. Of course you do."

"I don't know that I do," he said. "I am bonded to her. She is my twin. We are in many ways pieces of one. She is the head of the nation. And I have been her shield. That's different than love."

"What do you think love is?"

For a man convinced of his own rightness in the universe, his own deep sense of knowing who he was, a question like that was confronting.

Because when he dug down to the bottom of himself and searched for the answer, he found it wasn't there. "I don't know."

"Do you think that maybe it could be the way that you protected your sister. At the expense of yourself."

"No," he said.

"You don't think that love sacrifices itself?"

"If that is love, then love is a cruelty visited on the world. As cruel as hatred."

Her throat worked up and down. "Will you be involved with our child?"

"No," he said, something in his gut twisting, repulsion making his skin crawl.

"I don't understand, Gunnar. I don't understand why you would come for me like you did if you are not willing to offer me anything." She frowned. "Why did you come? How did you know I was pregnant?"

"I tracked your name in a database which attached you to that clinic. I knew why you must've gone there."

"You came to me knowing that I was having a child. And even now you can't bring yourself to admit that you might want to be in that child's life?"

"I don't know," he said. "I cannot explain what drives me. I don't like that. Not at all. I am a man who has always known how to stand firm in his convictions. I had to fight for those convictions. I had to fight my own father. I had to withstand torture. And I am not a man given to change, particularly not quickly. What I have always known is that I did not want to bring a child into the world, but now I am. Now we are. And what I know, with equal ferocity is that I cannot abandon the child." The words were like acid on his tongue, like sharp knives in his chest. "I don't know what love is. And I don't know how to be any sort of decent person. But I do know protection. I know I can offer that. And I offer it to you. To our child. I can pledge allegiance to you. To the baby. I don't know what I can give beyond that. But what I always want my child to know is that I will be a protector. Because Astrid and I never had that. Not from our father. I would have our child know he is loved. *I* don't know how to do that," he said, his voice raw. "I will need to count on you for that. For you to show the child that which I cannot."

She looked at him, and the well of pity in her eyes was almost too much for him to bear.

"Gunnar…"

"Forgive me," he said. "For what I said. I was angry, because I was afraid. And it gets me to say that. All of the things my father did to me and I was never afraid. But it's as if it was all stored inside of me for later. For when I was the one with power. Because I do not wish to use mine in the way that he did. And I thought it best… For the longest time, to avoid what I thought made him the monster he was."

"You thought somehow you made him a monster?"

"If I had not been born, then what choice would he have had? He would have had to accept Astrid. Power corrupts. And in me, my father saw the promise of power."

"I think you've proven that you're incorruptible in those stakes," she said, her voice soft.

"I have never trusted it. Why should I be innately better than my father?"

"Because you want to be?"

She sounded so confident and yet he didn't see how she could be. "Do you ever worry?" he asked. "After what your parents did to you, don't you worry that something inside of you might be broken?"

She looked so serene, and he could not understand it. He could not understand how this woman seemed so utterly and completely without fear for the future. For the child that she carried in her body.

"No," she said. "I worry about some things, but not being like my parents. That life didn't make me happy. And their goal was to have more of that life. They cared so deeply about what other people thought. They cared about power and prestige. I lived there, in that life, and it made me miserable. Their pursuit of more made me miserable. I understand that there is no value in treating people like a commodity. Because I understand not only that more things will never make me happy, but that it does unrelenting damage to the person that you put that on. I know everything I don't want to do. I'm sure along the way I will stumble upon more things I shouldn't do, or things I should do more of. I want to be the best mother that I can be. And I know that that begins with not being like my own. I was raised by nannies and teachers. I was raised by everyone but my parents. Their presence only served to make my life miserable. As they brought their expectations down upon me, as they told me all the ways in which I wasn't meeting them. No, I don't worry that I'll be like my parents. And I don't think you should worry you'll be like your father."

"But we have no guide," he said.

"Even if we did, that child will not be you, and it will not be me. It will be different than either of us, its whole own person. We would not be able to plan perfectly even if our parents had been wonderful."

"You won't use nannies?"

"Oh, I imagine we will to a degree. But we will be involved too. Not because we have to be, but because I want to be."

"What if I'm bad at it? What if it would be better if I weren't involved?"

"We can speak of that as the time comes," she said.

And somehow that was more reassuring than if she had simply told him that everything would be fine. Because the fact of the matter was she didn't know. Gunnar was desperately boggled by this uncertainty inside of him. It was nothing like he usually was, and nothing like he wanted to be at all.

That was the root of all that fear he'd felt when they had first made love without a condom.

Like the world had spun out of his control. And control had been his linchpin ever since he had been a boy, attempting to withstand his father's torture.

That deep base he had built inside of himself had been the only secure and certain thing. It was the thing he relied on. That internal compass. He had no idea how he'd come by it, because it certainly hadn't been taught to him by his father. He had no idea how he'd been so fortunate as to have something like that inside of himself. He had often felt like maybe it was part of that connection with Astrid.

At the very least, Astrid had had something more of a connection with their mother.

Their mother hadn't been interested in Gunnar at all, but she had cared deeply for Astrid.

He had always been grateful that his sister had that.

"We can figure it out together," Latika said. "And if something is going wrong, we can change it. We are not made of stone. Our ways aren't set. We can choose who we want to be. I believe that. All I wanted, all my life was my chance to choose my own path. I'll do so now. And so will you. We can do it. We are not bound by this. We don't have to be."

He didn't want to speak anymore. Not now. Instead, he reached out and picked Latika up off of the seat she was on and carried her over to the bed.

He was desperate for oblivion. He craved it. The future was a bright, blaring light of some uncertainty. Of so many things he had not planned. So many things he had always told himself he didn't want. The only thing he was certain of was that he wanted her. With a desperation that bordered on insanity. Yes, that he was certain of.

He stripped her bare, and he spent the rest of the night proving to her that while he might be uncertain about some things, there were others he was infinitely confident in.

For now, that was enough.

The future would have to handle itself.

CHAPTER THIRTEEN

THE NEXT FEW weeks went by smoothly. Latika felt at ease with Gunnar in a way that she hadn't ever before.

They spent their days companionably enough, Gunnar busying himself with work, but often including her in discussions about new projects. She enjoyed that.

It gave her a purpose.

One beyond dwelling on her current morning sickness.

It was really such a terrible thing, and she found that she could barely rise before ten a.m. Which was completely unusual for her. But she was living on unsweetened herbal tea and dry toast and crystallized ginger candies.

After all that settled, she could bring herself to rise.

She was thankful that Gunnar had suggested they come and live at the palace when they returned. Because that put her in proximity with Astrid very often, and, it meant that they had a whole range of staff available at all times, and given that Latika was currently feeling quite down, it was exceedingly helpful.

Physically, she might be diminished, but emotionally things were going better than she could've possibly asked.

She was having a fortunate moment when she went out onto the terrace to sit in a lounger, in the pale sun making a weak appearance in the pale sky.

That was when Gunnar came out to find her there.

"How are you feeling?"

She smiled, a strange, warm sensation flooding her.

Gunnar had told her a few weeks ago that he didn't know what love was.

Latika was beginning to think that she did. She felt that every time she looked at him. Every time she thought about him.

"I just wanted to come and tell you that I will be heading to San Diego tonight."

That startled her. "Why?"

"There's a big project opportunity, but there's been a snag with some of the planning. I need to see to it in person."

"Let me go with you," she said.

"There's no need," he said.

"Why not?"

"You don't feel well," he said. "In any way, you will be well taken care of here in the palace. And you will have Astrid around you. Wouldn't you prefer that?"

"Would I prefer your sister's company to yours?"

"She's your friend, after all," Gunter said.

"And you're my husband," Latika responded. "I'm not sure why you don't think that takes precedence."

"Ours is not a conventional marriage," he said. The way he said it, so casually, hurt her. And she knew that perhaps that wasn't fair. He wasn't wrong.

Theirs was not a conventional marriage. It never had been. She had thrown herself at him in a crowded ball-room and demanded his protection, when he was in a position of such public visibility he had no choice but to go along with what she done.

But over the past weeks their marriage had felt conventional enough. In fact, it had felt more than conventional. They had slept together, shared with each other. Grown together.

He had begun to feel like the most important, defining piece of her life.

With Gunnar, she had found something that she hadn't found with anyone else.

He seemed to accept her for who she was. More than that, he seemed to enjoy all that she was.

He shared his business information with her, and complimented her on the way her mind worked. He valued her mind, he valued her body. Every piece of her seemed important to Gunnar.

How could she feel anything but adoration for him?

He also got angry with her sometimes, and she liked that even better. Because it showed her that he could want her even when their interaction wasn't companionable. That he didn't require her to be perfect in order to want her company. In order to want to kiss her and pleasure her and be inside of her.

Everyone else had only ever wanted her on their terms, with the exception of Astrid, who had been her truest friend.

And in Gunnar, she had found a man who cared for her that way, and she could not understand why he might think that wasn't earth shattering.

"Our marriage might not be conventional," she said softly. "But it's important. I find that I'm not happy when you aren't around, Gunnar. And I should like to go with you to San Diego."

He regarded her, his expression unreadable.

"It would be best if you stayed home," he said.

"I don't understand. Why would you care either way?"

She suddenly felt very silly. Arguing over whether or not he should bring her. Truthfully, it was kind of sad. Because if he didn't want her there then she should just accept it. It was difficult to do, when she wanted him like she did. It was difficult, because she wished more than anything that he would crave her company in the same way she craved his. But if he didn't... Then, even if he agreed to bring her along it was something of an empty victory. No, it was more than an empty victory.

It was a loss, and she a bad loser. But she wasn't sure right then if she cared, mostly because she wanted to know why. Wanted to know why he was avoiding spending time with her.

Maybe he just needs space. And the fact that for you it's a revelation that someone wants your company some of the time is a bit more of a novelty for you than it is for him.

Perhaps.

Except, she knew all he had been through with his father. And she had a feeling that this wasn't an entirely familiar situation for him either.

"If you want to go by yourself, you can. But I'm not sure why you think I might be an impediment," she said slowly. "Unless there's something happening you don't want me to know about."

She truly didn't think that Gunnar would be unfaithful to her. She didn't know why she thought that. He had never once sworn his fidelity to her, beyond when they had taken their wedding vows, and at that time both of them had been lying, since neither of them had had plans to sleep with each other then.

"I'm not going to be manipulated, Latika," he said, his voice suddenly turning to shards of ice. "That was what my father did to me. Manipulation. All the damn time. And you trying to make me feel guilty, trying to make me feel concerned by the questioning of my character is not going to make me change my mind."

"I wasn't manipulating you," she said. She felt horrified that he might think that, but then she looked closely at his face, and she saw he lacked sincerity.

He didn't think that she was manipulating him. Not really. Not deep in his heart. And that meant he was the one doing the manipulating.

"What's going on? That is not a leading question, neither is it manipulative. But you're being strange. We've been close to each other these past weeks."

"We have been sleeping together."

"More than that. You swore to protect me."

"Leaving you in a palace surrounded by guards, and with your best friend is hardly walking back on my promise to protect you."

That was true enough.

"Well, then maybe it's more than that. Maybe I want more. Gunnar... I have always been surrounded by people who wanted to use me in some fashion. And you... It isn't like that with us."

"Latika, it is the very definition of that with us. You needed protection. I needed a way to improve my reputation. And so here we both are."

She couldn't do this. Not with him. She'd been on a quest for freedom, for the life that she would have been destined for if not for...well, if not for her life.

And that was the problem, she realized.

She couldn't be Latika without her past. Without the years she'd spent with her parents, then the years that followed in Bjornland. It had all been her life, and it had made her into the woman she was.

A woman who loved the man she had married.

She was not waiting on this. She wouldn't let him leave without him knowing.

"No. That was true when it first began. What we have now isn't that. It isn't for me. Gunnar... I've fallen in love with you."

He drew back as though she had slapped him. "No," he said, his voice like iron. "You don't love me."

"I do," she said. "I've been thinking a lot about that. What love is. Because you asked the other day. Because you said you didn't know. But I think... Gunnar, I think that you exemplify love more than anyone I've ever known. With no regard to your own safety or comfort you protected your sister. For no glory and no advancement. You shielded me from Ragnar, even though you could have easily acted like I was a crazy person throwing myself at you the way that I did."

"And put your life at risk? How reasonable is that?"

"Let me finish," she said. "And then you came for me. You came for the baby. Even though you didn't know if you could be a good father. Even though it terrified you."

"How can you possibly act as if I exemplified love in any way through those actions. You remember what I said to you. The night that we first made love."

"I do. I remember it well, because it hurt me. It hurt me deeply. But it wasn't the final thing you did. Those were words, Gunnar. You took the appropriate steps, the appropriate action to fix those words, and that matters more."

"But some things cannot be erased."

"No, but they can be forgiven."

"Just like that?"

"It isn't just like anything," she said. "But we've had weeks where you have demonstrated to me that the things you said that night were spoken in anger. Anger that came from a very understandable place of fear. You had a plan for your life, Gunnar, and this was in it. I understand that. And also, when push came to shove, you came for your child. You came for me. And since then, you have demonstrated all of those things I just said. And through it all, you've shown me what I want for my life."

"It's just another cage, Latika. Don't thank me for putting you in another cage."

"What?"

"You are…conditioned to make the best out of a bunch of very bad situations. You chose to be here, you chose to be Astrid's assistant because the alternatives to you were vile. And our marriage is no different. Now you find yourself with child, and you see the benefits to the two of us being married, over the benefits of us being separated. That doesn't mean it's what you would have chosen. With an entire world at your disposal. I was one of two options placed in front of you, and you took the one that would not result in your abuse and torture. And then, I presented you with very few options when I came to London to collect you."

"You didn't threaten me. And you gave me a great many opportunities to tell you no, if you don't remember."

"But I would have threatened you," he said. "If you

had not come with me, I would have threatened to take your baby from you. And I think on some level you knew that. I wasn't going to let you waft off into the distance with my child, disavow all connection of my blood with me. You knew I wouldn't allow it."

"I didn't know any such thing. I did not make the decision to go with you under duress. I left you under duress. I separated myself from you in San Diego under duress. I wanted to be with you. I was upset when you said those things to me because I wanted you to be a different man. Because the man that I saw hints and glimpses of was one that I knew I could fall in love with. And I wanted more of that man. Well, in the past weeks you have given it to me. And I... I would choose you. With the whole world before me. I would choose you."

"You don't know that."

"I do."

"You've never had enough freedom to be confident in that fact."

"By your standards, does anyone? Maybe only you. Except, even then you had your reputation to consider. Who chooses a partner with nothing in their life coming into play? Who chooses a partner with no consideration for anything? Very few people, Gunnar, so if circumstances make it so that my feelings don't count, then I would say that most relationships are invalidated. People find love. They find it in the strangest places. They find it in adversity. They have always done so. Whether it's because our hearts crave companionship, or because fate finds ways to wind our paths together no matter what, I don't know. But I know that love finds us. And it has found me. It has found me here with you."

"I don't believe in love," he said, his face hard like

stone. "And I certainly don't believe in it with the way things have happened between us. How can it be real? These are trying times, the have found us entwined. It's not fate, but a series of choices. Choices made out of desperation. Choices made by evil men. And none of them yours to be made freely."

"I just told you…"

"And I feel it is something you need to tell yourself. Because otherwise, here you are pregnant with my child and in a sense, it's just sadly inevitable. Because you weren't exposed to other men. Because you were never given the chance to marry another. Because a jailer without sadistic tendencies looks alarmingly attractive next to one who enjoys causing pain."

She would not let him win. She would not let him reduce her. She returned volley. "All of my life I've had people telling me what they thought was good for me. I won't let you do it too. You have trusted me. You gave me selection power over your bride in the first place. You showed me your business, and you've been consulting me on certain things. How can you now decide that I'm ignorant and know nothing?"

"All right, Latika, have it your way. You understand your heart. You understand your mind. You love me. But your love is misguided and misdirected. Because I do not love you. I cannot. Love means nothing to me, so if you're seeking to offer it as some kind of gift or prize, then I think you truly misunderstand who I am."

"How can love mean nothing to you? Look at Astrid. Look at how much she cares for you. And surely your mother…"

He cut her off with cold, decisive words.

"My mother knew that I was being tortured," he said,

his voice hard. "She did nothing. My *loving* mother. She didn't care one bit what my father did to me. Because I wasn't the child that mattered to her. I existed to be a pawn in my father's eyes. And I was nothing in my mother's. Do not ask me to cling to some source of love that believe me never existed."

Latika's heart curled in on itself. Pain lancing through her. "Your mother knew?"

"Why do you think…" He stopped himself, paused for a moment, before continuing. "Why do you think I am so certain that there is no part of me who would do well with a child? It doesn't come from nothing. My own family was so very broken, Latika. I have offered what I can offer. And beyond that…there is nothing."

"I don't believe that. I just don't. I believe there's more. I believe that you have more to give. I do. Down in my soul I believe it."

"Because you want to see this as something you can hope for. Because you want to see it as something you weren't trapped in. But you are. You are trapped, as am I. We are trapped with the child between us, and what can be done? You would have lies. You would lie to yourself. You would lie to me. You would try and make all of this something that you could latch onto. But it is just more of life's cruelty. You are a good woman, to be able to possess the power to feel the way that you do after what you have been through. But you have been shackled to a man who cannot. And there is no fixing it."

"Gunnar…"

"No. I'm going to San Diego. And while I am there I will go about my business as if we are not married. Do you understand me? I will be what I am. Pure. Through and through. And when the world sees that, they will not judge you for leaving me. And that is what you will do. You will leave me."

"What about your reputation?"

"I don't care."

"I thought it was for Astrid."

"Have I not pledged to you to protect you? To protect the child? This is how it will be done. I do not recall making it a discussion. Astrid will find her own way. She is resilient. And what I'm doing... It is simply a holdover from when I was a boy, taking on my father's torture in the name of keeping her safe." A sad smile tipped his lips upward. "Perhaps I was never truly protecting her. I sometimes wonder that. Perhaps she never needed me. For she had all the strength that she possesses now, and she had the protection of my mother. I thought that perhaps my mother saw me as a source of protection for her precious daughter. But I think more she accepted that I was a distraction from my father's rage. He decided to try and use me to do his will, and he found me immovable. And I suspect that my mother imagined it was just as well. I was a worthy sacrifice either way."

"So that's what you're doing again? Martyring yourself?"

"It would only be martyring if it was something I didn't want. And I never wanted this life. Not really. So which one is martyrdom?"

She didn't have an answer for that. Not really. All she knew was that in her heart she felt like she and Gunnar had something special. Something important. But he was standing there with his eyes cold telling her that they didn't. So perhaps it was true. Maybe he

did not care for her. Not even a little. Not even at all.
Maybe there were no feelings between them, and she
had been desperate to conjure them up. Because they
were together. Because she had shared her body with
him. Because he had given her a child.

"I love you," she said, the words broken. "And I don't
care about pride."

Suddenly, she was desperate, emotion clawing at her
chest. "I don't care about my safety. Please don't give
your body to another woman, Gunnar, it's mine. I love it
so much. I love you so much. You're mine, and I would
choose you every time. Every single time. And I hated
you on site because I knew that I could never have you.
Because I knew that a man like you was beyond my
reach. And maybe I did manipulate the situation asking you to marry me. Asking for your protection. But
your protection was the only one I wanted."

She took a deep, sharking breath and continued,
"I could have thrown myself at Astrid's feet. I could
have simply used my connection to her to keep myself
safe. But I didn't. I didn't mean to manipulate you, but
I did. And for that I must apologize, because I know
how much you hate it. But don't ever underestimate
the power of choice. Because I did choose you. I did.
We could go on all day about what my options were,
and why you were the best one. But I know in my heart
why you were the one I chose. Because you're beautiful. And brilliant. Because I was so enraged by your
exploits with other women because I was jealous. Because I found your beauty so magnetic and undeniable I couldn't turn off my response to you when we
were in the same room, and it terrified me. I want to
be with you," she said. "From now and until always.

When we took our vows I didn't know what I wanted. I was confused."

"You told me that you wouldn't sleep with me," he said.

"Because I wanted children. I was afraid. I was afraid that if I slept with you this would happen. And it did. I was trying to protect myself from the inevitable. Because I knew... Gunnar, I knew that part of you not wanting children was you holding back your emotions. Please don't give what we've shared to someone else. Please don't ask me to go."

"Where do you wish to live?" he asked, not responding to her at all. "I will establish your living quarters there."

"With you, you idiot. In your home, in your bed."

"Anywhere else in the world, Latika. It's yours. But not with me. Not here."

He tilted his chin upward. "I swore my protection to you, to the child, and I will give that. But I will give no more. I hope you will have found a new place to reside when I return. You will want for nothing. My word is binding. Because I never use them to manipulate."

"No. You do. You use them to manipulate yourself, Gunnar. And if you can't see that that I don't know how to help you."

But he said nothing to that. Instead, he turned and strode off the terrace, leaving Latika stunned. Because there was no more discussion. And he had simply walked away. From her. From this. From them.

And it all felt too unreal for her to even believe that it had happened.

But the stunning, intense feeling of being cracked from the inside that overtook her when she drew in her next breath told her that it had. She slid off the chair, on her knees on the terrace, gasping for breath. She had never felt like this before. Ever. And she thought she might be dying. She had run away from her parents, parents who had been intent on marrying her off to a madman. Had seen how little value she had to them.

She had hidden away for years, had been through so many things that should have done this to her. Should have immobilized her. Should have left her completely and utterly breathless with pain. And yet none of it had.

But this… This was beyond what she thought she could endure.

Always in her life when she had been backed into a corner, she had known that she had to move. Had known that she needed to take a step away from the threat so that she would be safe. But here she was immobilized. Because the man who had just hurt her far beyond anything she could have ever fathomed, was also the one person she wanted to be with more than any other. And she found she had for self-protection.

Because all of her walls were gone. She had fallen in love, and it had stolen all of her protection.

It had stolen everything.

And she had no idea how she was going to survive this.

But suddenly, she remembered.

She put her hand on her stomach, covering her body. The place where the baby grew.

The baby was why she would survive. Why she would carry on.

And more than that, why she would find ways to be happy.

Because she would never subject her child to an unhappy, bitter upbringing.

Her chance at love was this baby.

And yes, Gunnar had come and found her, and he had given her hope. But the loss of him didn't mean the death of her hope.

If she had learned one lesson through all of this it was that the amount of hope that existed in her was an incredible thing. She had grown up in a cloistered life, but she had hoped for more than what her parents had chosen for her.

She had hoped for more than a marriage without love.

That hope was strong. And it would carry her through, even when she couldn't carry herself.

That she had to rest on the strength of that hope, because more often than not it was the only strength available.

When Gunnar arrived in San Diego, he was something more than jetlagged. Something worse than hung over. He didn't understand the thing that was happening inside of him. He didn't understand why the hell he couldn't seem to think straight.

He'd needed to get away from Latika for a while. Because the days and nights of time spent with her had begun to erode the walls he'd built in his soul to protect himself and he'd begun to feel battle worn.

Not from torture or isolation.

From her soft touch on his skin. From her kisses on his lips.

And so he'd devised a trip to get away from her for a while and then...then it had all gone to hell.

Everything felt like it was wrong.

Muddled and messed up, and like it would never be right again. He had endured a great many things in his life. Things that would have broken many people. Most people. But he had never felt like he lost his purpose. He did now. He felt like he couldn't remember the reason he was supposed to breathe. Or a reason anyone might keep breathing.

The world seemed dark. Beyond dark. The world seemed like a completely and unutterably foreign and dark place. He could find nothing bright or hopeful in it. And in the past, when he had felt that way, he had been reminded that at least there was alcohol. At least there was sex. But the despair that he felt now could not be dealt with alcohol. And he didn't want women. Not any woman other than Latika. Ever. She was everything. And she was gone. He didn't know what in the hell he was supposed to do with that. Or why in the hell he had behaved the way he had.

Except.

Except. The thing she had been offering to him seemed far too good, far too good to be real. That was something he learned in life. That anything that seemed too good to be true was. The one time his mother had ever shown any interest in him was when he had been a boy. He had spent hours being tormented at his father's hands.

He had spent days confined to the dungeon. Kept in an area that was not large enough for him to lay down. He had been cramped and isolated, and when his mother had seen him again she had acted like she was glad to see him. And then it had become abundantly clear that she didn't wish to hold him or comfort him. But that she was only concerned that his father might have made some headway in convincing him to try and overthrow Astrid. To contest her position for the throne.

It had never been about him.

He had only realized later that of course, if it would have benefited her to liberate him from his father's clutches, she would have done so. But it didn't. Because if she had tried to get him over to her side, then it would perhaps inspire his father to use other means to get his way. And if she had exposed him to the public, well then... The entire reputation of the royal family of Bjornland would be at risk. And that was something that of course neither of his parents could ever chance. It was a terrible realization.

To know that his own mother had weighed and calculated that. That his own father had done the same. And given the way that his parents felt about him, he could not fathom that Latika could feel any different.

His chest felt crushed.

Was he really so simple?

Was he really so simple that he could not face her declaration of love because he feared he might be harmed? Because he feared all the weak and vulnerable places in him that it exposed. The kind of husband and father he could not be.

Because he could not expose himself to such pain.

He was a coward. And yet, he did not know if he possessed the strength to fight against his own cowardice. He was going to go out. He had every intention of going out. Of finding a woman and getting caught in a compromising position with her. Of destroying the reputation that he had built up for himself. Of breaking their marriage apart. Latika had begged him not to touch another woman, so logic dictated that the first thing he should do is go out and touch another woman.

Except the very idea turned his stomach.

He prowled through his house, empty.

This house that had always brought him such satisfaction. A place that he had built far away from himself and the legacy of his father. Yes, this house had been important to him. As had the fact he had built a business across the world. But now, it all seemed trivial.

Because for a while Latika had been in this house. And when Latika had been in this house, it had been something magic.

When he had taken her out against the wall in the terrace, and fulfilled the fantasy he'd had of tasting her as he'd done.

When he had taken her up to bed and taken her virginity. When her innocence had acted like a dagger and stabbed him through the heart. Had made him wonder whose blood it was that was on the sheets.

She made him feel things he hadn't thought possible, and he resented her for it.

He had never depended on another person. Not once in his life.

He knew that Latika loved him. Really, love wasn't the issue.

He didn't know how to need.

Because days spent in solitary confinement at the hands of his father had taught him not to. Because living with a mother who had cared so little for him, who had certainly never held him, not once when he had fallen, had informed him that he could not depend on anyone but himself.

But part of him thought he might need Latika.

And he didn't know what to do with that.

And then she would have a child, one that would need him in return.

He could not fathom it. He didn't want to.

It was painful. Utterly and completely to imagine the scenario, and almost worse to imagine the alternative. He needed her.

He didn't want to need her.

They were having a child. He was desperate for that child. He also didn't want to be desperate. And God help him if he knew what the hell he was supposed to do with either feeling.

He had done what he had become proficient in. Running away. Yes, he was very accomplished at that. It was what he had done, after all. The method by which he had handled his father. He had not exposed the old man—and perhaps the excuse that it might damage Astrid's credibility and harm her was valid enough—but there were other factors. Because it had been more satisfying, because it had been easier, to simply walk. To simply cut ties and care for nothing. To wave a red flag at the bowl in that regard. And to give himself reprieve.

He was a man who had made his own destiny, and who was very proud of it.

But a huge portion of that journey had been about twisting the problem to suit him, rather than killing it once and for all. Perhaps that was what he had done here. Perhaps that was what he had done with Astrid.

But he didn't know who he was, at the end of everything. Didn't know what he was actually capable of.

Because all he ever asked of himself was that he protect Astrid. That he survived.

And suddenly, it hit him like a wall of bricks.

He was accusing Latika of reacting because she had no choice. But he was the one who lived in that world. He was the one who had made every decision he had made because the alternative was so undesirable.

Who would he have been without the abuse of his father? If he'd not had to dedicate his whole life to protecting Astrid? Would he have wanted children. Would he have reacted to the news of Astrid's pregnancy with joy rather than with anger? When Latika had come to the palace to be his sister's assistant, would he have immediately allowed himself to fall for her? How different would everything have been? It was impossible to say. It was impossible to say, because they had not been given that opportunity. Because he had not been given that opportunity.

He put his hand in his pocket, felt the sensor that would start his car. He could go out. He could go out and he could make a scandal. He could destroy his marriage to Latika. It was one of his choices.

Choices. Yes, he had them. He could go back to Bjornland, he could confess his undying love, and what then? What then. What would happen when she tired of him. What would happen when he couldn't be what she needed him to be? In his experience, that meant that he was not worth the effort. And as a man who was not worth the effort, he simply could not believe that he was now.

He gritted his teeth, and turned, walking out of the apartment.

Yes, they all had choices.

And sometimes the choices before you were grim.

But he would do what he had to. To set them both free.

CHAPTER FOURTEEN

WHEN LATIKA CAME down to breakfast the next morning, Astrid's face was guarded.

"What?" Latika asked.

"It has to do with my brother."

Latika felt like a knife had stabbed her through the heart. "I assume you mean he's gone out and found himself a lover."

Astrid blinked. "Did you know he was going to?"

"He told me he would."

"Why?"

"Because I told him I was in love with him, and he did not find that to be satisfactory. But I also begged him not to do this. I told him that we…we could be happy together. We could be. I don't know why he is intent upon hurting himself. I feel…" She sank down into the chair, a tear sliding down her cheek. "Give me the paper."

Astrid pulled it toward her chest. "You don't want to see it."

"I should see it. I need to see it. I really do."

"I know. I would feel better if you didn't."

"Well, this isn't about either of us feeling comfortable."

Astrid slid the paper across the table. And there were

photographs. Of Gunnar with a blonde woman. He was only talking to her over drinks, but his hand was rested low on her back, and the headline implied that the two of them had left together. Trouble for the Royal marriage as the Playboy Prince was caught canoodling a California girl.

Latika surprised herself by grabbing the paper and balling it up, throwing it across the dining room.

"I told you," Astrid said.

"I've never been jealous before. It's awful."

"Yes," Astrid agreed. "Of course it's awful."

"I don't want to hurt like this," Latika said.

"Unfortunately," Astrid replied. "It does hurt when they break your heart."

"Like when Mauro broke yours."

"Yes."

"He didn't sleep with another woman."

"Gunnar might not have either."

Latika knew that was true. And in fact, it did make some sense. Because Gunnar wanted to drive a wedge between them, and he wanted to do something that he thought she might find irreversible. In this... Well, this would be that thing. So of course, it made sense that he might go to such great lengths.

"Maybe." She sighed. "He told me to be gone when he got back."

Astrid looked like she was made of steel. "No. That isn't fair. You don't have to leave. He's the one who should leave."

"Well, good luck kicking him out of his own palace."

"It's my palace. I was born first," Astrid said imperiously.

Latika's breath caught. "Yes."

"Why did you say it like that?"

Latika shook her head. "There are things that... There are things that Gunnar will have to tell you someday. But I can't break his confidence."

"Even now?"

"Even now."

Astrid sighed heavily. And then she stood up, both palms on the table. "Well. If you're bound and determined to be that loyal to him, then I suggest you stay. Stay in your bedroom. Keep your things there too. Refuse to leave. Whatever he needs to see... Prove to him that he cannot get rid of you."

"And if he did cheat on me?"

"Only you can answer that question."

Latika knew the answer in her heart. That no matter what, she was committed to him. Committed to loving him. That whatever actions he committed out of a desire to run...she would forgive.

She truly, truly hoped that she didn't have to. But she was willing. Because she loved him.

And she was tired of living a life where she made subpar choices to run from a bad option.

Gunnar was a good option. Even if he wasn't perfect. She didn't need perfect. She needed love.

And in the end, she would see to it that love conquered all. In the end, she would show him just how strong love was. She only wished that she didn't have to demonstrate it with quite so much intensity. But she would.

By the time Gunnar returned to the palace in Bjornland, he was prepared to find an empty bedroom where Latika should be. Because of course he had done what he needed to do.

He had gone out and found himself a woman. That he had betrayed their marriage vows. And why would she think he had done any differently.

Exactly the way he'd promised he would.

Or at least, made it seem as if he had.

In reality, nothing could have enticed him to touch the blonde woman he had spent approximately ten minutes chatting with. He had asked her to step outside with him, and she had complied. Then he had paid her a significant amount of money to walk away and not go back into the bar.

As he had anticipated, opinion pieces on his behavior began pouring in immediately. It was nothing more than he had expected. And nothing more than he deserved. And it would allow Latika to be free. Truly. She would be a paragon of virtue in the eyes of his people, and indeed, the people of the world. His child would know his father, and even if he had to spend a lifetime atoning for the supposed sins he had committed against Latika, the child would not be denied its parentage, and that, was something of absolute importance to Gunnar.

He had solved everything.

And yet, he felt empty.

He stood at the threshold of the palace in victory.

And yet, he felt defeated.

There was nothing to feel overly proud of. Not in this.

He moved through the corridors of the palace, managing to neatly dodge any of the serving staff, but when he went to the staircase that he knew would take him to his room, he was met by his brother-in-law. Mauro was standing on the stairs, his gaze dark, his arms crossed over his chest.

"I didn't expect a welcoming committee," he said.

"You should have. Of course you should know that I would be aware that you had arrived back at the palace. And that we have all seen the headlines."

"Yes. I suppose I should have realized you were monitoring the border."

"Even you can't go undetected when we would like to see you."

"Well, that's good to know. I'll add espionage and surveillance to the long list of my sister's skills."

"How dare you come back here?" Mauro asked.

"I'm sorry, are *you* of royal blood?"

"Not last time I checked. But I am married to your sister. And I am a faithful husband."

"As far as I know, infidelity is as storied a tradition as the grand Christmas ball that our family throws every year. My people have never much concerned ourselves with anything quite so pedestrian as keeping our vows. I'm not sure why I should be the start of that."

"Astrid and I are the start of that. And she thought well enough of you that you might continue it."

"Well, my sister is optimistic. Especially where I'm concerned. I am nothing immensely exceptional. She should not expect it of me."

He began to move past Mauro, and his brother-in-law planted a firm hand on his shoulder. "Explain yourself."

"I do not have to explain myself to a man such as you."

"Explain yourself," Mauro repeated.

"Sometimes the kindest thing a man can do is set a woman free. I would think you of all people would know that."

Morrow's face darkened. "Are you suggesting it would've been kinder for me to set your sister free?"

"No. But I know you thought that one time. And here you are. You are a good father. A good husband. A man that I am happy my sister has found a life with. But for a while you thought that would not be the case. And you did what you had to. I know myself. I know my heart. And what I have done for Latika was the kindest thing that could be done. Trust me on that."

"You were not here to see her distress. I was. You broke her. If you weren't such a coward that you ran to execute your plan, then you could have seen it yourself, and you could've told her that it was for her own good."

Mauro shook his head. "For my part, I cannot see how harming another person in that way could ever be for their own good."

"Why is it that you're speaking to me instead of Astrid?"

"Astrid didn't trust herself around you. She thought she might execute you."

Gunnar laughed, and then pushed past Mauro. In many ways, he would believe that was true of his sister. She was fearsome, and it was one of the things he respected about her. One of the reasons he had always felt it was important that she be the one who took over the throne. That she be protected at all costs.

But what about yourself?

It didn't matter. The choices were made. And they were done.

He had taken up his mother's charge, and even she had not sworn any kind of loyalty to him.

After of a betrayal such as the one he'd committed, there was no reason to believe that Astrid ever would.

As he continued down the corridor, a door opened, and his sister appeared. "We must talk."

"I just shook off your attack dog."

"Yes I know. Because I told him to speak to you so that I wouldn't have to."

"And yet, here you are."

"Because it's important. It's important that we speak. Latika told me that there was something I didn't know about you. And she refused to elaborate. She said she would not break your confidence. She said this to me even after she had seen the news of your betrayal. Because that is the woman that you have behaved so poorly toward. A woman who would protect you when you absolutely did not deserve it."

He shook his head, a grim weight settling in his chest. "Believe me, Astrid, the question was never whether Latika was good enough for me."

"What don't I know?"

"There is no point rehashing this. There is no point at all. Our lives are what they are. You have found happiness with Mauro, and I am glad for you. I don't need to bring my pain at your feet. My life is also established. It is set. I am what I was made to be."

He looked at his sister, who was like gold plated iron, and he realized he was selling her short. Her strength. Her wisdom.

He had always sought to protect her, but in many ways he had underestimated her.

As his father had always done.

And that…that could not stand.

"Then if everything is set in stone, you might as well tell me. If nothing can be changed…"

"You know how badly our father wanted me to be King."

Astrid stared at him, her eyes wide. "Yes."

"He sought to use me as a weapon against you. He wished to turn me against you. And his method of doing that was to attempt isolation. Torture."

The horror in his sister's eyes was everything he had been trying to avoid for the past twenty years. "And you can see now why I didn't want to tell you this. You can see now why I never wanted any of this."

"Why did you not tell me?" she asked, her voice a broken whisper.

"What purpose would it have served? I had to protect you. It was the most important thing I could do. I had to serve you. You are my Queen. You are my sister. And protecting you all this time has meant shielding you from just how corrupt our father was. Because what does it benefit you to know?"

"So that I could know you," she said. "Not everything is about me, Gunnar. And that is a sentence I never thought I would say to you. Because you have lied all this time about who you are. You let everyone believe that you were selfish. And instead, everything you did was for me. How could you let me go my whole life not knowing that?"

"Because I am still broken. And there is no fixing it."

"How are you broken? It was never you. It was them. All this time it was them. Both of them, Gunnar. Mom and Dad. Don't think I don't realize that. But I was the fulfillment of mother's ambition. And that you are clearly the attempted fulfillment of our father's. When we were lost in the middle. But look at how you have loved me. Look at how loyal you were. How loyal you are. Gunnar, you gave me things I did not deserve with your devotion. No one could possibly hope to deserve. Because how can a person deserve to have someone else sacrifice their safety and comfort for them? You can't. Something like that is never about deserving. It's about love. And love is never something any of us could earn. Not love on the level that you gave me. It is a greater love than most could ever hope to receive."

"I have never felt like I possessed any great love inside of me."

"Because you didn't just let it sit inside of you. You poured it out for me. Love is useless as a feeling. It takes on a new shape when it becomes action. And sometimes that action is a sacrifice, and there is nothing comfortable and sacrifice. But it's real."

"I never wanted to hurt you with knowledge of our father's treachery."

Astrid put her hand on her heart, as if it was in pain and she was trying to minimize that pain. "I'm not hurt for me. I hurt for you. For myself… I have never felt so loved, Gunnar. To have a husband who loves me as he does. To know that my brother loves me in such a way. I cannot fathom how I was born so fortunate."

Gunnar had never thought of it that way, and it was as if everything was turned upside down. That what he'd done for Astrid would make her feel not the betrayal of their parents, but the deep love that he felt for her.

And it was love.

He could see it now. The way that she'd spoken of it. Love that fills you up so very much that you had to pour it out. Love that existed somewhat uncomfortably because it demanded things of you that did not feel good or satisfying.

And now he felt he understood something about love.
Something that perhaps might have saved his marriage.

Except... Except what he had done to Latika... She
would not forgive him.

Though, he had not betrayed her, he had certainly
made the world believe he had. And even if he were to
try and fix it now, she might not believe him. And the
world certainly wouldn't. So she would always have to
be the woman who had gone back to a man that had
been unfaithful.

He had created for himself an impossible situation
and now, it was too late to fix it. She would be gone
now. As he had told her to be. Because he had broken
her. Mauro had told him that.

"Excuse me," he said.

Because whether or not it was too late, he was going
to try.

Choices. These were the choices. He could live forever without Latika, or he could try. Living without her
was unacceptable. And so he had to try, no matter how
unlikely it was that he would ever earn her love again.

But love was such a very precious thing, and Latika
had put her love for him into action. Had laid herself
bare. And that kind of love had to be rewarded. Because
that kind of love mattered. When he saw it through the
same lens that Astrid did, that bravery and that sacrifice... Latika had done all that for him. She had begged,
she had put herself before him raw and naked. And he
had given her so little in return. He would make it right.
He had to make it right.

He pushed his hands through his hair, making his
way down the hall and pushing the door open, expect-

ing to find that same sense of emptiness that had been in his San Diego home.

But instead, he saw her.

Latika was sitting on a bench at the foot of their bed, her long dark hair cascading over her shoulders, her expression set into one of seriousness. He could see that she had been crying. That he had made her cry. He had never despised himself more than he did in that moment.

"I thought I told you to leave," he said.

"You did," she responded. "And you did everything you said you would. You are a man of your word, Gunnar, I will give you that. But I didn't agree to leave you. And I won't leave you. I love you, and I want more than anything for this to work. And I know what they'll say about me. How sad I am. That I'm so desperately delusional for thinking that my husband who was unfaithful to me could ever change."

She shook her head. "I don't care. I don't care what anyone thinks of me. I'm not making decisions for other people anymore. I'm making decisions for myself. From my heart. And what's right for me."

"You would… You would stay with me even now?"

She stood. "Yes. I would. Because I fell in love with you, and I fell in love with each and every broken part of you. The broken part that made you feel you had to run. That made you feel you had no other choice but to try and undo this once and for all by sleeping with another woman. If I believe that love can heal, then I must give it time. I won't stay with a man who cannot love me ever. But if you think there is hope, that we can make a marriage work. That we can love each other, then I will stay. I am…devastated that you would give to someone else what we have shared. But I promise that I will do everything in my power to forgive. To never hold it over your head. I believe that you can be better. And if I believe that, then I need to give you the chance to be."

Her words nearly took Gunnar down to his knees. For what had he ever done to deserve such an offer? Such complete and utter loyalty. He had become his father in many ways now. He had tortured her. And yet, she held fast.

And then, he did find himself on his knees in front of her, taking her hands in his. "I don't deserve such an offer," he said, his voice rough.

"Love isn't about what you deserve," she said softly, her words so closely mirroring Astrid's that the truth of them rang through him like a gong.

"My darling, Latika. I don't know why you would choose to believe me. But I did not sleep with her. I didn't even kiss her. I made all the world think that I did, though, and that means that it will follow us. That means that…you will not be free of the insinuations that will come, and the outright, blatant commentary. And that will be my fault. For I have done that to us."

"You weren't unfaithful to me?"

"No. And I'm sorry that I let you keep talking, and keep thinking it. But I wanted you to understand that I wasn't telling you this to manipulate you into staying. If you would stay either way… And you know I have no reason to lie. I swear to you I wouldn't lie. Not about this."

"I believe you," she said softly. "I swear that I do."

"I was afraid. And I was running. And every single thing that I accused you of… I was the one who felt like I was stuck with a series of choices, handed down to me from others. And I realized that I was continuing to let my father manipulate and control my life. That I was allowing my mother to continue to have dominion over what I was."

He pushed his hands through his hair, and saw they were shaking. "I have always fancied myself a man who lived free. A kind of rogue prince who did whatever he wanted, but that isn't true. And it never has been. I let myself wonder…what kind of man would I have been if not for that?"

"A dangerous thing to wonder," she whispered. "We are what we were made."

"It's true, but I think, Latika, I would have chosen you much sooner. I love you. I don't need time to fall in love with you. I simply needed to find a way to rout the fear out of my heart so that I could give that love space to be felt. And more importantly, so that I could allow myself to act on it. I told you I didn't know what love felt like, but I have come to understand that it isn't important to know what it feels like. It is much more important to know what it looks like."

His throat tightened, making his words rough. "Because love that *feels* like much but looks like nothing is useless. You demonstrated deep and real love for me. The way you chose to stand with me, to be steady. When I was not. You offered me faithfulness when I appeared to have given you none, when for all intents and purposes, I had given you none. You demonstrated bravery in the face of rejection when I couldn't. And that, will always be what love is to me. And it is the love that I will endeavor to give back to you. To be brave when I feel afraid. To give when I feel like being selfish. To love when it would be easier to hate. I will make these choices for the two of us. I swear it. I swear it to you."

She threw her arms around him, a sob racking her shoulders. "I was willing to forgive you, but I'm so glad that I don't have to."

"You will still have to forgive me," he said. "Because whether or not the world will believe that I was faithful to you is another story. And our marriage may forever be tainted by the public perception of what I have done."

"I don't care about public perception. That is the only thing my parents ever cared about, and believe me, it never made any of us happy."

"I don't think I will ever elevate the nation. My reputation may be too far gone."

"Whether or not the world ever knows, you did elevate the nation. You protected their Queen. You protected me. I hope someday the world understands the manner of man that you are. But if they don't... I do. And I will ensure that our child knows it too."

Gunnar took her chin in his hand, stared down into her beautiful brown eyes. "I don't need the world to know a damn thing about me. As long as you trust in me, then I will be happy."

"I trust in you."

"Here I give you vows that I mean with all my heart," he said, holding one of her hands clasped in his. "That I will be faithful. That I would lay down my life for you, and our child. But I will reserve the realest parts of me for you. And only you."

"And I will do the same," she said, one small hand covering his. Then Latika stretched up on her toes and kissed him. Pure and sweet and more than he could have ever hoped to deserve.

But the beautiful thing about love, the real love that had surrounded him for longer than he had allowed himself to see it, was that it transcended what a man deserved.

The best things, Gunnar thought as he carried Latika to bed, were free. They were beyond price. They could not be bought, they could not be worked for, they could only be given.

And Latika had given him her love.

The thing that a man who could afford anything, who had been entrenched in a life that involves no denial, and no deprivation, had never known he was missing.

And as they came together, man and wife in every sense of the word, that hole that had always been there in his soul felt filled.

Completed by this woman. Completed by her love.

EPILOGUE

THE KINGDOM HAD rejoiced when Astrid had given birth to her son, the heir to the throne of Bjornland, but there was no less celebration for the birth of Gunnar and Latika's daughter.

The beautiful Princess with jet-black hair and eyes the same color as her mother's.

And when Gunnar and Latika renewed their vows in an intimate ceremony, attended only by Mauro, Astrid and their children, the photos—of the new baby, and of Latika in a wedding dress made of simple, rich satin, that she'd been so afraid to let herself wear to that first wedding—had helped cement the acceptance of the royal couple as one that would last.

A couple worthy of rooting for. Especially in light of the new revelations that had come to light over the past months.

Gunnar and Latika had been willing to figure out a way to address the issues he had created with his headline within their family. To make sure their daughter understood what Latika believed if ever the time came when she stumbled across those stories.

But Astrid had a different plan. Astrid took it upon herself to demolish the secrets and lies that their parents had lived with. The web of deceit and corruption that had surrounded the castle while they had been alive.

Of course, it had dashed her father's reputation. And it created many questions about the long history of their family.

But it had given the world the truth about Gunnar. About his loyalty to the crown. To his sister.

And to why he had contrived to make it look as if he was unfaithful to his wife.

And of course, there would always be people who believed that Gunnar was not a hero, but a villain involved in a desperate PR campaign.

Though Latika knew the truth. And that was all that mattered.

She knew, beyond a shadow of a doubt that she would love this man forever.

Prince Gunnar von Bjornland, her husband, wonderful father and the pride of his nation. A man she loved with every fiber of her being.

It would be her great joy to be his wife, for all the rest of her days.

* * * * *

LET'S TALK

Romance

For exclusive extracts, competitions
and special offers, find us online:

f facebook.com/millsandboon

📷 @millsandboonuk

🐦 @millsandboon

Or get in touch on 0844 844 1351*

For all the latest titles coming soon,
visit millsandboon.co.uk/nextmonth

Want even more
ROMANCE?

Join our bookclub today!

'Mills & Boon books, the perfect way to escape for an hour or so.'

Miss W. Dyer

'Excellent service, promptly delivered and very good subscription choices.'

Miss A. Pearson

'You get fantastic special offers and the chance to get books before they hit the shops'

Mrs V. Hall

Visit millsandbook.co.uk/Bookclub and save on brand new books.

MILLS & BOON